Confectionately Yours

Something New

Also by Lisa Papademetriou

CANDY APPLE BOOKS

Accidentally Fabulous

Accidentally Famous

Accidentally Fooled

Accidentally Friends

How to Be a Girly Girl in Just Ten Days

Ice Dreams

CONFECTIONATELY YOURS

Save the Cupcake!

Taking the Cake!

Sugar and Spice

OTHER NOVELS

Chasing Normal

Drop

M or F?

Siren's Storm

Sixth-Grade Glommers, Norks, and Me

The Wizard, the Witch, and Two Girls from Jersey

Something New

Lisa Papademetriou

SCHOLASTIC INC.

All activities in this book should be performed with adult supervision. The publisher and author disclaim all liability for any accidents or injuries or loss that may occur as a result of the use or misuse of the information and guidance given in this book.

ISBN 978-0-545-22231-0

12 11 10 9 8 7 6 5 4 3 2   13 14 15 16 17 18/0

Printed in the U.S.A.   40

First printing, August 2013

Book design by Yaffa Jaskoll

To Lila Templin

Stuck

"Come on, Meghan! It's not that bad! Just close your eyes." I try to sound encouraging. I also try to squash the laugh that threatens to escape in a snort-spray that would make my good friend furious.

"I can't close my eyes and come down a ladder at the same time!" Meghan wails.

"It's only five steps!"

"Hayley, I will *break* my *neck*!"

And that's when I do let loose with a little snort. I can't help it. The way she says "break my neck" sounds just like a clucking chicken. You know, "Bok-bok-bok!" Her bangs are dyed a brilliant yellow, which contrasts with the natural peach of her red hair, which only adds to the chicken effect.

Meghan glares at me. "It isn't funny! I'm stuck! I'll be stuck up here forever!"

"Meg, you're, like, four feet off the floor. It's not like you're at the top of the Empire State Building!"

Laser Beam Death Ray — that's the look she gives me. Maybe I should have been more sympathetic, but she's just stuck at the top of a bookstore ladder. Seriously. I think my toilet is farther off the ground than this ladder is, but she's clinging to a shelf of self-help titles as if it's the side of a cliff.

"The Empire State Building doesn't bother me," Meghan says. "Short heights are worse for me than tall ones."

"Why did you go up that ladder in the first place?"

"I was looking for cookbooks for *you*!" She holds up a hot-pink book titled *Cupcake Carnival*. "You could at least be grateful!"

"I am," I tell her, which is true. It was sweet of her to try to get me the book. My mom and grandmother run a tea shop, and I do a lot of the baking. Cupcakes are kind of my thing. "Thanks for putting your life in danger for me."

"So what are you going to do about it?" Meghan demands.

"Well, if you're going to be stuck up there forever, I guess I could bring you sandwiches."

Meghan holds up the book as if she might hurl it at my head, but there is laughter in her hazel eyes. That's the thing about Meghan Markerson — she has a really good sense of humor. She can definitely appreciate when she's being a lunatic. Not that it stops her. "So that's it?" she demands. "No dramatic rescue?"

I sigh and look around the store. We're in Crow's Nest, the best — and only — used bookstore in downtown Northampton. The woman behind the counter is as thin as my dental floss and has long gray hair. It is unlikely that she would be able to lift Meghan off the ladder. It's clearly up to me to make something happen. "Oh, all right," I say, starting up the ladder.

"What are you doing?" Meghan demands.

"Piggybacking you out of here," I tell her.

Meghan looks horrified.

I turn my back to her. "Just hop on," I say. "You can close your eyes."

"You'll drop me!"

"I'm incredibly strong."

"No, you aren't! You're extremely feeble! Besides, I wouldn't even let the Hulk carry me off this ladder!"

"Fine, then. Get used to living up here." I start back down the steps.

"No, wait wait wait!" Meghan cries. "Okay, okay!"

I plant myself on the step before hers and turn my back. Meghan begins to squeal, but she wraps her arms around my shoulders. Then she transfers her weight onto me, and I start down the steps, with her draped across me like a blanket. Three more steps. Two more.

"Awesome!" someone shouts.

I look up to see Omar Gutierrez snapping a photo of us with his smartphone. "One for the school website!"

A vivid image of how absurd we must look flashes through my mind. It must have flashed through Meghan's, too, because she screeches, "Omar!" and the moment my feet hit the floor, she drops the book, then leaps off my back. "Give me that camera!"

Omar laughs and sprints through the store, and Meghan races after him.

Omar is a prankster, and he's tangled with Meghan before. My guess is that she's going to make him pay for that picture. I pick up the baking book that Meghan dropped, and flip through the pages. It has the basic cupcake recipes, like vanilla and chocolate, but it also has some interesting ones, like avocado and papaya. Really pretty pictures, too, and instructions on making frosting decorations. The price is reasonable: three dollars. I decide to get it.

I head to the cash register as Omar blasts out the shop door and onto the street. Omar is the number one base stealer on our school's baseball team. He's fast.

"I'll be back," Meghan calls to me as she races after him.

"Take your time," I tell her, but she's already gone.

"Well, that was exciting," says a warm, gravelly voice. Mr. Malik is standing in front of the cash register, holding a slim book with gold lettering on the cover. "The thrill of the chase," he adds, with a familiar twinkle in his black eyes. He hands his money to the cashier.

"I don't think it's really that thrilling," I tell him.

The creases of his face dance into a smile. "Oh, there's nothing so thrilling as young love."

That makes me giggle. Mr. Malik owns the flower shop beside our tea shop, and there is no doubt that he's a romantic. "Believe me, Mr. Malik, those two are *not* in love."

"There's a fine line between love and hate," puts in the wiry woman behind the register as she rings up Mr. Malik's book. Not that anyone asked her.

"In this case, it's less of a line and more of a barbed-wire fence," I reply.

"Ah." Mr. Malik's chuckle is like a tiger's purr. He hands over the money and smiles sheepishly at the cash register lady. "Well, I suppose I just have love on my mind, then. And speaking of love," he says, handing me the book he just bought, "would you mind delivering this to your dear grandmother?"

"Sure," I say, blushing a little. Mr. Malik has been my grandmother's friend for years, and they just got engaged. I am still trying to get used to thinking of him as my almost grandfather. "*The Collected Poems of Livingston Wells*?" I say, reading the title.

"An excellent poet," Mr. Malik says. "One of England's treasures."

I nod. The name is familiar. I wonder if Gran already has a copy of this book.

The door bursts open, and Meghan blasts in. Her eyes are narrowed, and she's breathing hard.

"Did you get him?" I ask.

She holds up a finger and continues to pant. Then she puts her hands on her knees and leans over. "He's so fast!" she gasps. She lies down on the floor.

"Please don't block the doorway," the cash register lady says.

Meghan rolls away from the door and continues to stare up at the ceiling. I go and sit beside her. "I got him," she says between gasps. "He promised he wouldn't post the picture."

"Lucky you," I tell her, and she shakes her head.

"He's so *fast*," she says again.

"So are you," I point out. "You caught him. And you're wearing *clogs*."

Meghan groans. "Worst trip to the bookstore ever."

I hold up my two titles. "Not for me."

"Good-bye, Hayley!" Mr. Malik calls as he pushes open the door. "And farewell, dear Diana! Good luck on your hunt!" he says to Meghan.

Meghan watches him leave, then turns to me. "Doesn't he know my name? I've met him about five hundred times."

I have a feeling that Mr. Malik was referring to Shakespeare or Greek myths or something, but I decide to just say, "Probably a brain malfunction. Everyone gets them."

"True." Meghan hauls herself to her feet and brushes herself off.

I stand up, too. "Did you see the picture?"

Meghan shakes her head. "Omar claims he deleted it."

"Do you trust him?" I ask.

"Well — I guess we'll see."

"Right," I say.

Only time will tell.

Confession:
We May Have Lucked Out

It's lucky that Omar was on his own. He usually goes everywhere with his best friend and permanent shadow, Jamil. And Jamil would have definitely posted the picture online.

Then he would have made color printouts and posted them all over town.

Then he would have submitted it to the yearbook.

Don't get me wrong — Jamil isn't mean. But he really can't help pulling every prank he can think of. It's just his personality. It's like, you can't blame an ant for showing up at your picnic, can you? Or a cloud for raining on you? That's just what they do.

Omar isn't exactly like that. At least, he wasn't like that before he started hanging with Jamil.

I guess we'll find out what Omar is like.

One way or the other.

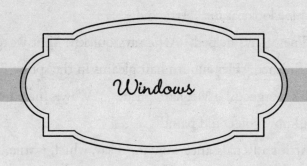

Windows

"*W*hy are they staring in the window of the Tea Room?" Meghan asks as we walk down the street. We're still a few doors away, just passing the new Mexican restaurant that recently opened up, but I can see my little sister, Chloe; her best friend, Rupert; and my ex–best friend, Artie, standing in a clump. They're all frowning at the window the way people frown at art in a museum. Like they're thinking about it.

People don't usually think about our windows.

It's a beautiful day out, and the sidewalk is crowded with people enjoying the sun. They keep having to go around the Window Starers. Three steps later, I can finally see what they're all gawking at, and I let out a little gasp. "Who did that?" I ask.

Chloe looks at me. "Artie did."

"These guys helped," Artie says quickly. "But we're not quite finished." Her auburn hair gleams in the spring light.

"It's gorgeous!" Meghan gushes. "Wow! Incredible! I didn't know you could paint!"

"Artie's a Renaissance woman," I say, which is true. Artie is a terrific singer, dancer, actress, and painter. And she also gets straight As. And she's really pretty.

It was never easy to be her friend, to tell you the truth.

Now she has painted our windows with a Beatrix Potter–style tea party. Flopsy, Mopsy, Cotton-tail, and Peter are all seated around a table, eating delicate little cupcakes and pastries. Mrs. Tiggy Winkle is brewing tea on a nearby old-fashioned stove. It's really cute and cozy looking.

"It needs something," Artie says.

"Maybe someone could be coming through the front door," Chloe suggests. "Like the Easter Bunny! Maybe carrying a basket of dyed eggs or chocolates or something."

Rupert shakes his head and shoves his glasses up on his nose. His dark eyes are huge behind the lenses. "The Easter Bunny isn't textually accurate," he says.

That's the kind of thing Rupert says.

"What does that mean?" Chloe demands. "Easter is three weeks away!"

"He means that these are all Beatrix Potter characters," Artie explains. "We can't just stick the Easter Bunny in there — it's too random. Which I kind of agree with. What do you think, Hayley?"

Artie turns toward me, twirling a thick strand of hair around her finger. It feels a little strange for Artie to be asking my opinion. She's my ex–best friend, but we've stopped hating each other recently. I don't know if we're exactly on the path to becoming best friends again. But it seems like we're off the path toward being dire enemies.

"I think the Easter Bunny is a cute idea," I admit, "but Rupert has a point. What about Benjamin Bunny, though? He could be carrying a basket."

"Perfect!" Artie says. "Done," and she heads for her brushes.

"I love it," Meghan agrees.

I'm a little worried that my sister will be disappointed her idea isn't going on the window, but when I look over, I see she's already moved on. Chloe bends down to pet a little white dog. Its hair is wiry, sticking out all over its body like a bristle brush. It has one floppy ear and one that stands straight up. This is one seriously raggedy-looking dog, but Chloe is petting it and cooing over it like it's cuter than a baby panda.

"Cutie, cutie, cutie!" Chloe sings out. "Cutie patootie!" The dog rolls over onto its back and puts its feet in the air while its owner — a man in a baseball cap — laughs.

"That dog has charisma," Rupert says, which makes me giggle.

I hold up Mr. Malik's slim poetry book and say, "I'm heading inside to give this to Gran."

Meghan is watching Artie paint the latest character into the corner near an unfinished doorway. "I'll be right there."

The café is crowded with people having murmured conversations and working on their laptops. Mrs. McTibble waves to me from her usual corner, and I wave back.

"Gran?" I call.

"Oh, hello, Hayley dear!" My grandmother pops her head out from behind a giant bouquet of roses and lilies that is stationed by the cash register. I could guess who those are from. "Look what Uzma brought by!"

Uzma is Mr. Malik's sister. She's a force of nature, and has been helping Rupert by taking him to school in the mornings and bringing him to our place in the afternoons. She and Gran haven't always gotten along, but lately, they have been growing on each other. "I absolutely adore star-gazer lilies." Gran breathes in the scent of the large pink blooms with the red center.

"I ran into your fiancé," I tell her, handing over the book. It's kind of fun to tease Gran about being engaged.

"Oh!" she says, turning pink. But when I hand her the book, her eyebrows pull together, and she sucks in her breath, as if a sharp pain has just stabbed her.

"Are you okay?"

Gran's blue eyes meet mine for a moment, and pause there. It's like she isn't looking at me, but through me, to something far away. "Thank you, dear," she says, placing the book on a shelf beneath the cash register.

It doesn't seem quite right. I'm about to ask if she's sure, when the bell over the door jingles and Meghan bursts into the café.

Meghan is always bursting into places. She never just walks, like the rest of us.

"Artie's going to help with the decorations for the fling!" Meghan does a little victory dance, a booty wiggle and finger snap thing.

"That's great," I tell her. "What are we talking about?"

Meghan stops her dance and gives me a look that could freeze water. "The Spring Fling Barbecue," she says slowly. "The seventh grade puts it on every year? I've been looking for someone to help out."

"Oh." Meghan is our seventh-grade class representative, so she's in charge of putting on a lot of events. "Okay. But, uh — are you sure it's a good idea to work together?" Artie and Meghan have a "special relationship."

And by that I mean, "they drive each other nuts." They tried to put on a talent show together, and it didn't exactly work out. Like, *Ka-Boom!*

"We might both lose our sanity," Meghan admits. "But I know Artie will do a good job, so that's all that matters."

"Would you like to have a few cupcakes for this event?" Gran asks, her eyes sparkling at Meghan.

Meghan clears her throat. "Well . . . ," she says playfully, "I was just about to volunteer Hayley for some baking." She pokes me in the shoulder. "You know you want to!"

I look over at Gran, who is smiling in this dimply way she has. "Sure," I tell Meghan.

"It would be our very great pleasure," Gran says. She's English, and can get away with saying things like that.

If Artie is going to be helping Meghan, maybe it's a good idea for me to be involved, I tell myself. Just to help keep the peace. Besides, I like baking cupcakes. I don't really need an excuse.

Meghan points to the paper bag in my hands. "Should we look at your new cookbook?" she suggests.

"What else are we going to do with it?"

But even as Meghan and I head over to a table to flip through the cookbook, I think about Mr. Malik's poetry book lying silently beneath the cash register.

And I wonder.

Confession:
I Know Where I Saw That Book Before

$\mathcal{I}$ just remembered.

It used to sit on the far left middle shelf in the living room. But it had a dust jacket. The dust jacket was dark red, with gold lettering that matches the lettering on the cloth cover that you can see now.

Gran used to read from it a lot. Before we moved in with her, sometimes Chloe and I would come over for a weekend visit. In the evenings, Gran would read us a poem or two. I remember part of one:

> *Remember that beneath the snow and ice,*
> *A world awaits, till winter's fury spent.*

I always thought that was a great poem for the end of winter, when you're really ready for the ice to break up and unleash the grass below. I know Gran loved it, too.

It's so amazing that of all the books in the world Mr. Malik would choose that one. It seems so romantic.

So — why isn't Gran happy?

Madhouse

"Sorry I'm a little late, Mom." She's seated on the hard wooden bench in the front hall of my school, and I plop down beside her. Around us, the hallways rattle and crash as students slam lockers and dash for the bus. Usually, I would be dashing, too, but I have a dentist appointment.

Mom peers toward the sixth-grade hallway. "Why are people shrieking?" she asks.

"A toilet in the boys' room overflowed," I explain. "Half the hallway is freaking out."

Mom grimaces. "That's disgusting!"

"It happens a lot," I tell her, and she looks even more horrified. "Really, it's not a big deal. They always get it cleaned up. The sixthies are just being dramatic." Just then, a little

test — if you do well on it, you can get college credit. Mom is usually really enthusiastic about anything college-related, but this time, she sighs.

"It's just . . . money's a little tight right now. And this says that the book costs over a hundred dollars." She doesn't look at me when she says this. She looks straight through the dashboard. Ever since my parents got divorced and my mom got laid off, money has been an issue. She's helping Gran by managing the Tea Room now, and it's going okay, but we aren't exactly planning a European vacation right now. Or even a trip to Goshen, where we used to go every summer.

"I know it's expensive."

Mom folds up the letter and puts it in her purse. "I'll think about it, sweetheart. I'll talk to your dad and see what we can do."

"Thanks, Mom," I say.

The car coughs and starts up, and Mom slowly merges into traffic.

Here's the thing about money: People always say that it can't buy happiness. But I'm not sure that's exactly true. I don't think being rich guarantees that you'll have a perfect life, or that being poor will make you miserable. But I know that not having money means you have to miss out on things sometimes. And not all of those things are shallow. Sometimes, they're important things. But you have to miss out, anyway.

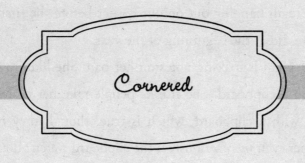

Cornered

The large sugar maple on the seventh-grade corner is already pale green — just starting to leaf out overhead. It's as if it has just started to wake up and think leafy thoughts, but hasn't gotten to work making real leaves yet. At the edge of our brick school building, a hedge of yellow forsythia gleams bright against the dull grass, damp and dirty from the retreating snow. It's still cold, but the light out is springlike, which warms me up somehow. Thirty-four degrees in March doesn't feel the same as thirty-four degrees in December. I don't know why. Maybe because everyone's so busy thinking about the end of winter.

So it's cold, but everyone kind of has the idea that it isn't, so we're all hanging out on our corner before the first bell, like we did at the beginning of the year.

Meghan is making notes on her pad. She likes to carry around a clipboard. She thinks people take her more seriously with a clipboard, which is true, though they might take her even *more* seriously if the clipboard weren't hot pink and covered with Hello Kitty stickers. I'm just saying.

"Okay, I think we've got food covered for the Spring Fling," Meghan says, checking something off with a purple pen. "You've got dessert. Artie is going to help with decorations and centerpieces. But I still need to get something for the drinks —"

"I have a big cooler," Marco offers. "I could bring that." Marco is one of my best friends and used to be my next-door neighbor.

"That would be great!" Meghan makes a note of it. "And maybe some ice?"

"Sure. I can take photos, too, if you want." Marco is an excellent photographer.

"That would be great! We could post them —"

"Hey, Meg!" Omar is loping toward us, his huge back-pack bouncing against his back as he runs. "Meg — I need to talk to you."

Meghan narrows her eyes as Omar joins us. "Why?" She really manages to pack that single syllable full of suspicion.

"What's up, Omar?" I ask.

"You're class rep, right?" Omar turns to Meghan. He slings his bag from his shoulder and plops it onto the damp ground. "Look, I have this idea for a tutoring program. A lot of people are having trouble with algebra, and I thought that maybe some of the kids who are really good at it could volunteer to help out. People could sign up, then meet at the library during lunch, or maybe at one of the back tables of the cafeteria."

"Hey, great idea," I say. "We could do other subjects, too." I'm thinking I could help some people with Spanish.

"I could use some help in English," Marco mutters.

"Right!" Omar grins at me. *Omar's actually a really good-looking guy*, I realize, *with his huge brown eyes and golden skin.* I just never think of him as handsome because he's such a pain.

"Hmm," Meghan says.

"Would you help me?" Omar asks. "I think we'll probably need to clear the idea with the administration and stuff, especially if we want to use the library."

Meghan gives Omar a little one-shoulder shrug. "It sounds like a good idea. Let me think about it."

Think about it? I'm really surprised. This idea seems so . . . Meghan-ish to me. I'd expected her to be all over it.

"Oh." Omar looks a little disappointed. "Sure. Think about it and let me know, okay?"

Meghan doesn't even say, "Okay," or anything, she just nods. Then she sort of looks at Omar from under her eyelashes until he grabs his backpack and walks away.

"What's up?" I ask as soon as Omar is out of earshot. "I thought you'd be into that idea."

"I am," Meghan admits. She starts doodling on her yellow pad. "But you know Omar. I'll do all the groundwork, and by the time the administration clears the whole thing, Omar will have forgotten all about it." She draws a star. Then another star. Spike after spike until her margin looks like a bush full of thorny burrs.

"I'll bet a lot of other kids would be into the idea, though," Marco says. "Even if Omar flakes out."

Meghan huffs out a sigh, which sends her bangs fluttering. "I've already got a million things to do."

"Just get another super organizer to handle the sign-ups and everything," I suggest.

Meghan barely looks interested. "Like who?"

I scan the clump of seventh graders on the corner. *Not Ellie Fisk*, I think. *No way would Oscar Chang be interested. Danielle Fitzgerald doesn't do anything but watch TV. Hmm . . .* My eyes land on a girl wearing an orange jacket and dark skinny jeans. Her hair is up in chopsticks. "What about Sadie Sunrise?"

Sunrise isn't Sadie Sunrise's last name — it's her middle one. But everyone calls her "Sadie Sunrise" or just "Sunrise." That's what happens when you have a super-cool middle name. My middle name is Claire, which is fine, but not exactly nickname material.

Meghan's eyebrows fly up. "That could work. . . ." she says slowly.

"Yeah, how come Sunrise isn't a class officer, or anything?" Marco asks. "She's the type. She's all organized with those perfect binders."

"And the excellent handwriting. Plus, everybody likes her," I add.

Meghan taps her purple pen against her lips. "Hmm. Maybe I should get her to run for student council with me," she says. "Maybe she'd like to help with the Spring Fling Barbecue, too!" Then, all of a sudden, she darts off to talk to Sunrise.

I turn to Marco. I'm smiling — I'm about to congratulate him on his excellent idea — but before I can say anything, Marco says, "Hey, Hayley . . . about the Spring Fling Barbecue . . . do you want to go together?"

Last year, Mr. Forbes, our science teacher, told us about this woolly mammoth that had been found by scientists in the Arctic Circle. It was perfectly preserved in ice. Like, the Ice Age had just come and — *zap!* The woolly mammoth was frozen solid.

Well, that's how I feel. Totally frozen solid, out of the blue.

Marco is one of my best friends. And he kissed me once. But that never turned into anything. So now he's asking me to this dance, and I don't know what it means. Is it as friends? Or is it some kind of date thing?

But there he is — my good friend, looking at me hopefully with his familiar dark eyes. Behind me, the bell to start school rings, and I feel the students, who had been littered across the front lawn and lining the walkways, all start to move as one toward the building. I have to give him an answer.

So I say the only thing I can think of.

"Sure, Marco," I tell him. "Of course I'll go."

Papaya Chocolate-Chip Cupcakes
(makes approximately 12 cupcakes)

I know that when most people think "tropical," they don't think about cupcakes. But they should! Here's a recipe that's good for an early spring day — when you're thinking about the warm summer ahead.

INGREDIENTS:
    1-1/2 cups all-purpose flour
    1 teaspoon baking powder
    3/4 teaspoon baking soda
    1/4 teaspoon ground cinnamon
    1/2 teaspoon salt
    1 cup papaya puree
    2/3 cup granulated sugar
    1/4 cup coconut milk
    1 teaspoon vanilla extract
    1/3 cup canola oil
    1/2 cup semisweet chocolate chips

INSTRUCTIONS:

1. Preheat the oven to 350°F. Line a muffin pan with cupcake liners.

2. In a large bowl, sift together the flour, baking powder, baking soda, ground cinnamon, and salt.

3. In a separate bowl, stir together the papaya puree, sugar, coconut milk, vanilla extract, and oil. With a whisk or handheld mixer, add the wet ingredients to the dry ones a little bit at a time, stopping to scrape the sides of the bowl a few times, and mix until no lumps remain. Then fold in the chocolate chips.

4. Fill cupcake liners two-thirds of the way and bake for 20–22 minutes, or until a toothpick inserted in the center of a cupcake comes out clean. Transfer to a cooling rack, and let cool completely before frosting.

Banana Frosting

INGREDIENTS:

- 1 cup coconut flakes
- 2 tablespoons butter, softened
- 2 cups confectioners' sugar
- 1 teaspoon vanilla extract
- 1/4 cup super ripe banana, mashed
- 1/2 cup mini chocolate chips (optional)

INSTRUCTIONS:

1. Scatter the coconut flakes on top of a baking sheet (preferably with ridges around the edges) and put in the oven to toast until they turn golden brown. Keep a careful eye on them, and occasionally stir them so that the coconut browns evenly. It will happen quickly, so be careful! Set the browned flakes aside to cool.

2. In a large bowl, with an electric mixer, cream the butter until it's a lighter color, about 2–3 minutes. Then add 1/4 cup of the confectioners' sugar and combine completely.

3. Add the vanilla extract and slowly beat in the rest of the confectioners' sugar in 1/2-cup batches. When all the confectioners' sugar has been added, beat in the mashed banana. Turn the mixer on high speed and beat for about 3–7 minutes, until the frosting is light and fluffy.

4. OPTIONAL: Mix in mini chocolate chips with a spoon for extra yumminess.

5. Frost each cupcake, add the toasted coconut flakes on top, and serve!

You'll Never Guess

"Should we guess the flavor?" my father's girlfriend, Annie, asks as I walk into the dining room with a large platter of cupcakes.

"You never will," Chloe says, lifting herself onto her knees in her chair. Chloe is in third grade, and small for her age. She usually sits cross-legged or on her knees, otherwise her legs dangle six inches from the floor.

"Well, yellow frosting is a clue," Dad says, scratching his salt-and-pepper hair. "Vanilla?"

Chloe huffs, as if she's insulted by the uncreative answer. That makes me laugh a little, because it isn't as if Chloe made the cupcakes.

"Oh, that's too easy," Annie says. "Something more original. The cake is pink — rosewater, maybe?"

"Still way off," Chloe replies.

"They're papaya chocolate-chip," I say, "with banana frosting."

Everyone lets out an "Ah!" and I hold out the platter to Chloe first. Of course, she chooses the largest cupcake.

Annie's long fingers reach for the prettiest one. It's funny how — in a batch of twelve cupcakes — there's always one that comes out looking worse than all the others. And there's always one that comes out looking better. And of course Annie spotted it. She's into pretty things — she dresses beautifully, her nails are always perfectly done, and her black hair always gleams. She even helped my dad pick out some stuff for the apartment. When he first moved in, it was pretty . . . blank. He had a bed and a desk and even a TV with a recliner in front of it, but there wasn't anything on the walls. After six months of dating Annie, there are ferns and paintings and floor lamps. Even curtains. In fact, the apartment kind of looks like a page in *House Beautiful*.

Dad picks a cupcake at random, and then I take one and

sit down at my usual spot. The dinner dishes have already been cleared away — Annie and Dad made pad thai — and Chloe put out the dessert plates. But mine is now covered with a large white envelope.

"What's this?" I ask. I pick up the envelope and move it off my plate so I can put down my cupcake.

"Open it and see," Dad urges. He takes a big bite of his cupcake and lifts his eyebrows at Annie, who smiles.

I lift the flap and pull out a brochure. Well — it's bigger than a regular brochure. It's more like a magazine, with thick, heavy paper. There are several pictures on the front: A girl with glossy blond hair and blinding tennis whites hits a ball. A serious-looking girl with glasses and dark cocoa skin frowns at a Bunsen burner. A muscular boy with a sharp profile shakes hands with a man in a tie. I recognize the man. He's one of our senators. *Islip Academy*, reads the headline. *Creating Leaders*.

I look up at my dad, unsure what to say. "Um, thanks for the brochure?"

"What is it?" Chloe asks, peering across the table. "What does it say?"

I look at my little sister. "'Islip Academy. Creating Leaders.'"

"Oooh!" Chloe's mouth drops open. "Oooo — ooooh!"

Dad laughs. "Hayley, I thought you might be interested in checking it out."

"Why?" I ask.

"Because it's one of the best schools in the whole country, Hayley," Dad says. "Wouldn't you like to go there?"

I look down at the brochure. "Isn't it a boarding school?"

"They have day students," Annie explains. "You don't have to live on campus." She tosses her long, gleaming black hair over her shoulder. With her elegant rose-colored silk shirt, porcelain skin, and shiny hair, she looks more like one of these perfect, perfect Islip students in the brochure than I do, even if she's twenty years older.

"Let me see!" Chloe darts out of her seat and comes to stand beside me. She plucks the brochure from my hands and starts flipping pages. "They give all the students a laptop!"

"You have to pay for it," I say.

"It's included in the tuition," my dad explains. "They have great science labs, and an excellent drama department —"

"Dance!" Chloe points to a photo of students at a ballet barre.

"I know — I was looking at that, too," Annie says with a laugh. "I want to go!"

"But — I like my school," I say.

Dad leans back in his chair. I drop my eyes to the uneaten cupcake on my dessert plate, but I can feel my father studying my face. I don't want to say what is really on my mind, which is the $130 for my Spanish book.

I know my mom mentioned it to my dad. I overheard her telling him while they were on the phone. And she also told him about the dentist bill. They share the cost of all that stuff. But the difference is that my dad has tons of money. He took a new job a couple of years ago, and his salary — which had been pretty low as assistant district attorney — suddenly shot up. Then, about six months ago, his law firm made him a partner. That was when all the new furniture and home décor appeared.

So. I wasn't sure what Mom would think of private school when she was worried about buying a textbook.

"This school goes through high school. If you go starting next year, you'll be all set." My dad leans his elbows on the table.

"It would be hard to leave your friends," Annie says gently. "But education is more important, don't you think?"

Annoyance pricks at me. Annie is nice, but she often just doesn't get me. It's not like it's her fault. She really tries. Anyway, I'm irritated that she thinks I just don't want to leave my friends, when there are really a lot of reasons I'm not sure about Islip.

"Why don't you just think about it?" Dad suggests. "Look through the brochure, and maybe we'll go check it out."

Chloe has already wandered back to her seat, her nose still buried in the pages of the Islip brochure.

I don't want to get into a big argument, or hear more reasons why I should want to go to one of "the best schools in the whole country." So I say, "Sure, Dad."

Kind of the way Meghan humored Omar.

And then — topic over — I eat my cupcake.

Confession:
Sometimes My Dad Forgets

$\mathcal{L}$ike I said, my dad and my mom have this agreement: They split a lot of expenses when it comes to me and Chloe. Like back-to-school clothes, junk like that. Usually, my mom will just pay for the stuff with her credit card, and then my dad can reimburse her.

The problem is that sometimes my dad forgets.

Two months ago, he forgot to send a check to cover Chloe's class trip. Mom freaked out a little bit because her credit card wanted her to pay a penalty, and it was, like, two hours on the phone for her to get everything fixed with them.

Not that she told me about it. But Gran's apartment over the Tea Room is pretty small, and I overhear a lot. I figure out a lot, too.

My dad isn't a bad guy, but sometimes he doesn't take care of things. Especially money things. It might be because — for years — Mom wrote all the checks, had all the bills set up online. She made sure everything was paid. So Dad isn't used to paying attention to that stuff.

But, also, I'm not sure he really realizes just how bad off we are. He knows that Mom lost her job, that she had to pay the mortgage on the house for a while after that, and that we moved in with Gran. But I don't know if he's *thought* about it.

I like to think that he *hasn't* thought about it.

It's better than thinking that he just doesn't care.

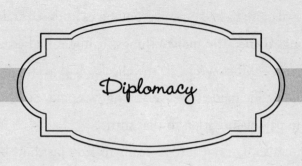

Diplomacy

"What makes these fish Swedish?" Meghan asks, pointing at the tub full of red gummy candy. "How can I tell if they're truly from Sweden? Like, what if these fish are being misrepresented as Swedish, and they're actually Norwegian? Do they have little fish passports?"

"It's kind of the same thing as with French fries, I guess." Luckily, I don't have to worry about whether or not my fish are Swedish. When it comes to candy, I don't usually go for the gummy varieties. I mean, I might buy a gummy worm to stick on a cupcake that's covered in Oreo cookie crumbs, like a garden. But if I'm just buying candy to eat, I go chocolate all the way: malted milk balls, M&M's, Reese's Peanut

Butter Cups — that whole food group. "Why don't you get some gummy sharks, instead?"

"And cause a breakdown in international relations?" Meghan demands. "I don't want to get reported to the United Nations!" She scoops a small school of limp fish into her plastic bag.

We carry our bags of candy up to the register. The high school student behind the counter barely glances up from the graphic novel she's reading as she pokes a button on the electronic scale and weighs our candy. I hand her a few badly crumpled bills, and she counts my change with one hand — she won't let go of that graphic novel.

Meghan swings open the heavy oak door and stands aside to let me through. It's a bright, clear day, and the moment I step outside, I let out a wild sneeze.

"Bless you," says a familiar voice.

Omar is standing on the street corner, holding a leash that leads to a dog that looks like a Doberman that might have been owned by a Munchkin. It has short black fur, a long-snouted brown face, comically floppy ears, and comes up to Omar's shin.

"Puppy!" Meghan says, leaning over to pet the dog.

"Actually, she's a full-grown dog," Omar explains. "She's a miniature pinscher."

"So — a little Doberman?" I ask, keeping my distance. To be honest, dogs scare me a bit.

"Well, she looks like it, right?" Omar says, smiling down at the dog. "But this breed is actually closer to a Jack Russell terrier than a Doberman."

"Is this your dog?" Meghan asks.

"No — I volunteer at the animal shelter," Omar explains. "This one needs to go out and get socialized."

"She looks pretty social to me." The dog wiggles happily beneath Meghan's enthusiastic petting, then sits up daintily, eyeing her candy. "Sorry, doggie," Meghan says. "These aren't dog treats."

Omar reaches into his pocket and holds out his hand. The dog nibbles the brown lump he offers, then prances around, hoping for more. Omar pats her on the head. "Maybe later," he says. Then he stands up and turns to Meghan. "So — Meg — Marco told me you talked to Sunrise."

"Yes! And she's going to run for vice president! Isn't

that great?" Meghan holds out her bag of candy, offering some to Omar.

"What?" Omar's head draws back in surprise, but he takes a red fish from the bag. "Thanks."

"We're a ticket! I'm running for president, and she's running for veep!" She does a little jiggy dance, then bites the head off a gummy fish.

Omar looks at me.

"I don't think Omar's talking about the election," I tell my friend.

"I thought you were going to talk to Sunrise about my tutoring idea," Omar says.

"Oh!" Meghan stops mid-chew. "I forgot all about that!"

I put a hand over my face as Omar's dark eyes smolder like hot coals.

Meghan squirms. "I kind of got sidetracked planning the election strategy —" She looks to me for help. "You know, we had to think about what to put on the posters and stuff. . . ."

"Making it worse," I mutter, shaking my head. Sometimes, Meghan doesn't know when to stop talking.

"Meghan," Omar says, "it's been a whole week!"

"Well, I wasn't even sure you were still going to care about it in a week," Meghan admits.

"Of course I care!" The little dog pricks up her ears, then prances over Omar's feet. He scratches behind her ears absently. "There are people who need help!"

I crunch into a malted milk ball.

"Okay, okay, Omar. I'll mention it to Sunrise."

"How do I know you won't forget again?" Omar demands.

"Oh, come on," Meghan says. "Why are you making a huge deal out of this?"

Omar's eyes narrow, and for a moment, I think I see a spark in them, as if the smoldering coals are about to catch fire. "Why are you acting like the election is a bigger deal than tutoring?"

"Because it is!" Meghan twists the neck of her plastic bag, as if she's trying to strangle it. She looks at me. "Right, Hayley?"

"Um," I say.

"Hayley, you're with me on this one, right?" Omar demands.

Actually, I am. But I don't really want to say so. Meghan is my good friend. "Uh — I think I'll just be a Swedish fish on this one." Omar looks confused, so I wave at Meghan's candy. "Neutral. Like Sweden."

"Isn't that Switzerland?" Meghan asks.

"Who cares?" Omar demands. "The point is that you said you would do something and you didn't do it! You're more worried about your dumb election!"

"Look, Omar, I'm not going to drop everything just to do what you want," Meghan shoots back.

"Isn't that what a president is supposed to do?" Omar demands. "Stuff to help the class?"

"Okay — I'll take care of it when I'm class president."

"And maybe you won't," Omar says. "Maybe I should run for president, so I can make sure things happen."

"Oh, please." Meghan looks at him over the top of her glasses. "Are you serious? You've never organized anything more complicated than a prank."

Omar presses his lips together and gives Meghan the kind of look that could melt plastic. "You don't know as much about me as you think you do," he says.

"I know as much as I need to," Meghan snaps. "Look, I'll help you, Omar, okay? Just let me get through the election first. We can start the program next year."

"That's too late," Omar says.

"What's the rush?" Meghan demands.

But Omar just shakes his head. The little pinscher has spotted a Great Dane lumbering down the street a few stores away and is straining at the leash. "Forget it," Omar says. "I'll see you around, Hayley." He lets the little dog lead him off.

Meghan bites her lip and sucks through her teeth as she watches him go. "Why didn't you back me up?"

"You could've at least *mentioned* the idea to Sunrise," I say. "I thought you were going to."

Meghan sighs. She holds up her candy, letting the bag spin, loosening the stranglehold on the neck. "I should have," she admits. "You're right."

"So — are you going to apologize to Omar?" I ask her.

"What? No way! That guy —" She rolls her eyes, not bothering to finish the thought.

The light changes, and we start across the street. "It should be an interesting election," I say.

"What do you mean?"

"If Omar runs for president," I explain.

Meghan stumbles a little as we step up onto the curb. "He was just kidding about that," she says.

"He was?" He sounded serious to me.

"Omar couldn't run for the *bus*, much less for president." Meghan's long green skirt swishes around her legs as she storms up the sidewalk.

"I hope you're right," I tell her. *Omar's a pretty popular guy*, I think. *It could be a tight race.*

"Of course I'm right," Meghan insists. "That guy." And she chomps down on another fish. Have you ever seen someone chew angrily? I imagine that poor candy fish is getting seriously mangled.

I sigh. Well, anyway, I hope Meghan isn't giving up on the tutoring thing. It really is a good idea.

But I know better than to say so.

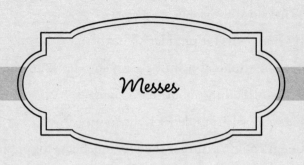

Messes

The café is bubbling with activity as I thumb through my new-to-me cookbook and crunch on malted milk balls. I'm thinking that a malted milk ball cupcake might be cool, but there are a few ideas in the book I want to try first. Meghan definitely picked a good one.

"Getting some ideas?" Artie places a mug of cocoa on the table across from me and then sits down. Just like that. As if it was something she does every day.

"Uh, yeah," I say, clearing space for her. I've been making some notes, and my papers are covering most of the small wooden tabletop. All the larger tables are taken.

"Don't worry about it," Artie says. "I'm used to dealing with your papers."

"I'm not as bad as I used to be." In my old house, in my old room, my desk was a total disaster. Open books, pages torn from magazines, tubes of glitter glue that I'd left open until they solidified, orange peels — you could find almost anything on my desk. As long as you weren't looking for my homework. Artie always thought it was funny, because I'm generally a pretty neat person. The rest of my room was usually tidy. "I share a room with Chloe now, so I can't be a slob."

"How's your messenger bag?" Artie asks with a knowing smile.

"Let's not talk about it." She has me, as usual — my bag is a disaster.

"Remember that time I found a six-month-old baloney sandwich in your desk?"

"That never happened," I insist.

Artie laughs. It *did* happen, and she knows it. The really gross part was that some creature had eaten part of the sandwich by the time she found it.

I tap a pile of papers on the table, straightening them.

"What's this?" Artie asks, reaching for the brochure that has just been revealed under my papers. "Islip Academy?"

She opens the glossy pages and starts flipping through them. "Wow, fancy."

"It is, kind of," I admit.

"Whoa — they have a sailing team?" Artie's right eyebrow lifts into a delicate arch. I have always envied her ability to do that. "And fencing!"

"Yeah. Did you see the labs?" I point out the picture of the gleaming black granite lab tables and all the chrome equipment. "They even have an observatory."

"No way."

"It's a small one."

"But still!" Artie's hazel eyes are glued to the brochure, where there is an image of a girl photographing a butterfly in a colorful garden. Below is the caption, *Summer enrichment photography class in the Shakespeare garden.* "Marco would kill to take a class like that," Artie says.

"Yeah."

Artie looks up, and our eyes meet for a moment. Part of the reason Artie and I stopped being friends is because she had a crush on Marco . . . and she found out that he had kissed me. We have both had crushes since then — both on Devon McAllister. But Devon turned out to be a jerk. I never think about him anymore, and I don't think that Artie does, either. But I wonder now if she still has a crush on Marco. Has it evaporated, disappearing into the air like steam? Or does it still linger, like a scar that remains even after the wound has healed?

Artie's eyes drop back to the page. "You should tell him about the class."

"Maybe I will," I tell her. *And, by the way, Marco asked me to the Spring Fling Barbecue.* I want to say it, but I can't make it come out. It seems . . . dangerous. Even though I feel like I should tell her.

I pick up the brochure and drop it into my messy, messy bag.

"So — what are you doing with an Islip brochure, anyway?" Artie takes a sip of cocoa. She's the only person in the world who can do that and not get a chocolate mustache.

"My dad wants me to think about Islip."

"Think about going there, you mean?"

"Yeah." I squeeze my shoulders to my ears and drop them.

Artie takes a long sip of cocoa and looks out across the café. "That would be too bad," she says, half to herself. Then she looks back at me.

"I know," I admit. I run my finger along the smooth, lacquered edge of the table, wondering if she means that it would be too bad . . . now that we're not fighting anymore.

"What are you doing Saturday?" Artie asks suddenly.

"No plans."

"Game Night?" she suggests. Surprise makes me choke, and Artie backs off immediately. "Oh, well, if you don't want to —"

"No," I say quickly. Game Night was something we used to do with Marco. All three of us would get together and watch a movie and/or play a game. For years, we spent our Saturday nights hanging out in my family's basement. But then I moved, and everything got weird. Still — Game Night is something I miss. "I'd love to hang out on Saturday," I say.

"Okay," Artie says.

And even though she's drinking from her mug of cocoa, I can tell she's smiling.

There's a tap on the window, and we both look up. Omar is outside with the little dog he was walking the other day, and he's gesturing wildly.

Artie takes a cool sip from her mug. "What's Omar flapping about?"

"I think he wants to talk to me. I'll be back in a minute." My chair squeaks as I push away from the table. "Hey, Omar — what's up?" I ask as I step out onto the street. I fold my arms across my chest and shiver a little. The sun has disappeared behind a pale gray blanket of clouds, and the air is damp and cold.

The dog sits at attention at Omar's feet and gazes up at me, as if she might have something to say. "Listen, Hayley, I'm sorry," Omar says. "I shouldn't have tried to drag you into that argument with Meghan."

"It's okay," I tell him. To tell the truth, I'd almost completely forgotten about it. But Omar winces, as if the memory is still poking at him.

"It's just — Jamil is having a lot of trouble in math," Omar admits. "I'm worried he might flunk if he doesn't get his act together."

"He doesn't care about school much," I say.

"Right. He's definitely smart, but —" Omar shakes his head. "Things are pretty rough at home, too. His dad is really hard on him." He stops and looks at me, as if he wants to make sure I'm understanding.

I don't really know what to say, so I just nod.

"He's a clown, but that's not all he is," Omar says.

"And that's why you care so much about the tutoring," I say. "But why not just get a tutor for Jamil?"

"No way. He'd never go for it. It has to be something normal — something that a lot of kids are doing. He hates to feel dumb."

"He isn't dumb."

"I know that. And you know it. But his grades don't show it. And his dad —" Omar stops, like he doesn't really think he should say more. I understand. These aren't really his secrets to be sharing.

"I won't tell anyone," I say. "But I'll push Meg to get behind the tutoring program."

"I'll do it myself, if I have to," Omar says, and his voice is like a promise.

"Eeee!" The Tea Room door bangs open and Chloe rushes out, trailed by our mom. And she plops right down in front of the miniature pinscher and starts patting her. The dog jumps up and licks her cheek, and Chloe giggles. She scoops the dog into her arms like a baby doll.

"Oh, she's cute," my mom says.

"I saw your doggie through the window!" Chloe exclaims.

"Oh, you're so soft!" The dog wiggles happily, licking her arm.

"She isn't my dog," Omar explains. "I volunteer at the animal shelter."

"I love dogs!" Chloe gushes. "So — wait — is this dog up for adoption?"

Omar grins as my mother says, "Oh, no."

"Please?" My little sister gives my mom the Big Bunny Eyes look.

"No, absolutely not." Mom shakes her head, but she doesn't sound as firm as she should, in my opinion.

"But look at how sweet she is!" Chloe insists. Now even the dog is giving my mom the Big Bunny Eyes.

"Chloe, we have a small apartment —" Mom says.

"Well, this is a small dog," Omar points out. "And you could think about fostering her instead of adopting."

"What's the difference?" I ask. I'm not liking this at all.

"You would just take care of her for a while, until the shelter finds her a new home," Omar explains. "The shelter loves to put the dogs with families whenever they can. The dogs are happier, and it makes the transition to moving them to their forever home easier."

"Did you memorize the brochure?" I ask Omar, just as Chloe says, "Yes! Fostering! We can foster the dog, Mom!"

"Well . . ." Mom is thinking about it, I can tell.

"Mom, dogs are a lot of work," I say. Chloe glares at me, and I wince. I know how much she loves dogs, but . . .

"I'll do it!" Chloe insists. "I'll take care of the dog! I really will! I'll do everything!"

"You can always bring the dog back to the shelter, if you're having problems," Omar says. "You're just fostering, not providing a permanent home. It's temporary!" And he shoots his gleamy white-toothed grin, and Chloe and the dog have their Big Bunny Eyes on, and Mom only holds out for about three seconds.

"Oh, all right," Mom says at last.

Chloe gives a shout and the dog starts to bark with happy, excited yips, and Omar claps Chloe on the back, and just like that — we have a new family member. Well, sort of like that. Omar can't just hand the dog over. He has to take her back to the shelter and we have to fill out paperwork and everything, but it's happening.

It's happening.

Lord help me; it's happening.

Confession:
I Remember Omar's Old Dog

Omar used to have a dog. Its name was Alabama.

As you know, I'm not wild about dogs, but Alabama was sweet and moved slowly. He was a black dog with a gray muzzle and watery brown eyes, and his tail would wag slowly back and forth whenever he did anything — greeted a stray dog, ate a treat, stopped to sniff.

He must have been very, very old, because his walk was jerky, like his joints needed oil. One day, I saw Omar carrying him down the street. The dog wasn't wriggling or trying to get away, or anything — he was just patiently letting Omar haul him around.

"Taking your dog for a walk?" I joked.

But Omar didn't laugh. "Well, he made it up the street,"

he said. "But I don't think he can make it back." He pressed his cheek against Alabama's ear, and Alabama licked Omar's face. Omar didn't say anything else. He just carried the dog very carefully across the street toward home.

Northampton is a small town, but it has a lot of creative types. It's not unusual to see people on the street doing something peculiar. You might see someone hooping with multiple hula hoops, or a dad and a baby sporting matching green Mohawks. A kid carrying a dog didn't register as interesting for most people.

But it was interesting to me.

Because Omar can be a pain . . . but a guy who loves his dog that much can't be all bad.

Quick Moves

"Who moves to Baltimore?" Meghan demands as she drops her lunch bag on the table and clatters into her seat.

"Is this one of those games where the answer is in the form of a question?" I ask her.

Meghan is so upset, she's practically vibrating, like heat shimmering on pavement. "Sunrise is moving to Baltimore!"

I nibble my sweet potato fry, which is just the right combination of salty and sweet, crunchy and soft. It's hard to get upset when you're eating something this good. "Why is she moving to Baltimore?"

"Her mom is going to head up some school out there," Meghan says, as if it's completely absurd for someone to take a new job in a different city. "Now I have to get someone else to run for veep!"

"Too bad," I say. "Sunrise would've been perfect."

Meghan rips the aluminum top off of her yogurt, then stirs it like she's out for revenge.

"You don't really need a running mate," I point out.

Meghan takes a bite of yogurt and looks out the window, thoughtful. "It's raining out."

"It's spring." I nibble another fry. "It's always rainy in spring."

It's an offhand comment, the kind people make all the time, but Meghan looks at me with her clear blue gaze. "Flowers need rain," she says.

"Yeah."

"Just like I need an organized person for vice president," Meghan explains.

"Hmm," I say. "Are those two things related?"

"I can run by myself, but I'm not sure I'd be a great president unless I could work with someone good for vice president. My ideas can't *bloom*, Hayley, unless I have some help!"

I make figure eights in my ketchup, thinking it over. "Well, maybe you should ask Omar."

"Omar!" Meghan tries to snort, but it comes out a cough, and she ends up hacking all over the table.

"Don't cough on my fries," I tell her. "Yes, Omar. He's smart, and he's pretty organized."

"No."

"And he really cares —"

"No," Meghan snaps. Her voice is like a door slamming. "Look, Hayley, I know you're trying to help. But Omar won't take being vice president seriously. Trust me. I need someone more like you."

The word *you* hangs in the air there, buzzing like a dragonfly, and Meghan's eyebrows lift.

"I don't think so," I say.

"Yes! You! Why didn't I think of it before?"

"I'm not really the student government type."

"Of course you are!" Meghan insists. "You helped me with the campaign to keep bake sales in school."

"Which totally failed!" I point out.

"But still! And you helped with the talent show."

"Because you made me."

"Well, I'm making you again!" Meghan grins. "Oh, come on, Hayley. Look — it'll be fun! I'll do most of the work, anyway. You can just help me keep on track. You're good at color-coding things — and at coming up with good ideas."

I feel like my mom must have, with Chloe and Omar and the dog all begging her to give in. "Oh, boy."

"Look, Hayley. It's mostly throwing parties. You love parties!" Meghan smiles sweetly. She interlaces her fingers and props her chin on them, batting her eyelashes.

Here's the problem: I can't think of a good reason to say no. If Meghan were president, we probably *would* have fun putting on parties together. And she has a point — I do enjoy color-coding things. I get that from my mom. "Okay, Meghan, I'll think about it."

"I knew you'd do it!"

"I said I'd think about it!"

"Oh, that's as good as saying yes. So we should probably start thinking about your campaign speech."

"Speech?"

"I'll let you see what I've written for mine, and then I'll help you work on yours. Okay, look, we have to submit your name to the office so they can put you on the ballot!"

"Wait — I never said —"

But Meghan has already darted off. To the office for my paperwork, no doubt.

It's amazing how some people manage to get a yes even when the answer is no. What's the trick to that?

And why hasn't anyone ever taught me?

Avocado Cupcakes

(makes approximately 12 cupcakes)

Avocados are nature's butter! They're just so creamy and delicious . . . and I always like putting something green into my cupcakes. It makes them seem healthier somehow.

INGREDIENTS:

1 cup milk

1 teaspoon apple cider vinegar

1-1/4 cups all-purpose flour

1 teaspoon baking powder

3/4 teaspoon baking soda

1/2 teaspoon salt

3/4 cup granulated sugar

1 teaspoon vanilla extract

1 cup ripe avocado, mashed (about 1 medium avocado)

INSTRUCTIONS:

1. Preheat the oven to 350°F. Line a muffin pan with cupcake liners.
2. In a large bowl, whisk together the milk and apple cider vinegar and let sit for a few minutes to curdle.
3. In a separate bowl, sift together the flour, baking powder, baking soda, and salt.
4. Once the milk has curdled, add the sugar, vanilla extract, and mashed avocado. With a whisk or handheld mixer, add the dry ingredients to the wet ones a little bit at a time, stopping to scrape the sides of the bowl a few times, and mix until smooth.
5. Fill cupcake liners two-thirds of the way and bake for 18–20 minutes, or until an inserted toothpick comes out clean. Transfer to a cooling rack, and let cool completely before frosting.

Super Quick and Easy Chocolate Buttercream Frosting

INGREDIENTS:

- 1-1/4 cups butter, cubed and softened
- 2-1/4 cups confectioners' sugar
- 1 teaspoon vanilla extract
- 2 tablespoons milk
- 3 ounces unsweetened chocolate, melted and cooled

INSTRUCTIONS:

1. Add all the ingredients to a food processor at once. Pulse to combine, and then process until the frosting is smooth.

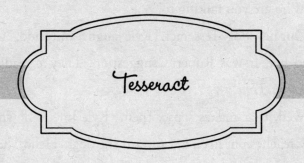

Tesseract

"Come on, Tessie," I say, giving the leash a gentle shake. It turns out that our new foster dog is a sniffer. Right now, she's smelling a tent pole for all it's worth. I wonder what it smells like. What could be so interesting? Did a squirrel rub up against it or something? I shake the leash again, but Tessie won't budge. I glance down at the list Mom gave me. If this dog and I don't get a move on, the farmers' market will close down around us. "Come on, girl."

"Fred?" A boy with curly blond hair turns away from a bucket of flowers to smile at me.

"Hey, Kyle. Yeah, it's me." Kyle is legally blind. He can see shapes and colors, but sometimes he needs a little help identifying faces.

"Who are you talking to?"

"Our new dog. Tesseract." Kyle laughs, and I add, "Chloe named her. It was Rupert's suggestion. They're reading *A Wrinkle in Time*."

"Well, that makes sense, then." Kyle kneels down and slowly reaches out his hand toward the dog. "Hello," he says softly. "Hi, Tessie."

Tessie stops sniffing the tent pole and starts sniffing his fingers. Then she starts licking them.

"Hah! I just had fries," Kyle says. "I must be pretty delicious."

"Nice and salty," I agree.

Tessie finishes licking him and puts her paws on his leg to reach up and sniff his nose. Kyle sniffs back. I'm over being afraid of our little dog, but I'm still not one of those people who likes getting licked and having a dog breathe in my face and stuff. Sometimes, I think I'm the only person in the world like that. I wonder if it's genetic or something.

"What brings you to the farmers' market?" Kyle asks.

"Mom sent me for some greens, and to see what other veggies they've got. But there isn't a lot here."

"It's early in the season. You could have some rhubarb."

"Right." I look around. "Or some baby plants. What are you here for?"

"I might get a couple of plants. I have a tiny garden. It's, like, three square feet," Kyle admits. "Mostly, I just like coming here to smell stuff."

I laugh. "Is the farmers' market smelly?"

"Totally smelly," Kyle says. "Didn't you know?" We're standing by a long table covered in plant starts. Kyle runs his fingers over the leaves and pinches off a leaf, then lifts it to his nose. "Lemon verbena," he says, holding it out to me.

I smell the leaf, inhaling a sharp citrus smell. "Wow — it smells just like lemon!"

"It's good in tea." He feels around the plants and pinches off an oblong leaf. He smells it first, then hands it over. "Lavender."

"Mmmm. This smells like my grandmother's fancy soap."

"Is it the kind of soap you're never allowed to use?"

"Exactly. It's in a pretty dish next to the towels we're never allowed to use."

"We have some of that. For display only." Kyle's gray eyes twinkle. I know he can't see me well, but he's really good at making me feel like he does.

He picks off a few more leaves, always careful to take one from the larger plants. Rosemary, chocolate mint, garlic scapes, each has a distinct, pungent smell. It's funny that I've never paid attention to that before.

It's amazing how being with a blind person makes you look at things differently. Or, experience things differently, I guess.

We fall into step toward the maple table. They have maple syrup, maple candy, maple cream, and brooms made from maple wood. A familiar figure in a purple miniskirt, hot-pink top, and plaid tights is buying a maple cookie. "Hey, guys!" Meghan chirps. "Look — they've got gluten-free cookies! Am I lucky, or what? Hayley, speaking of, do you think you could make a couple of GF cupcakes for the barbecue?"

"Sure," I tell her. "That's easy."

"Thanks! You're my GFF!" Meghan takes a bite of her cookie. "My gluten-free friend!"

"What barbecue?" Kyle asks.

"Kyle! The Spring Fling Barbecue! Haven't you seen the posters?" The words fall out of her mouth, and she freezes, then blushes a brilliant red.

"Meghan!" I squeal.

Kyle just laughs, though. "Wow — no. How did I ever miss them?"

"I'm such an idiot!" Meghan wails.

"You're fine, Meg," Kyle reassures her. "Don't worry about it. Hayley, could you just grab me a maple lollipop?"

"Sure." I take one and hand it over as Kyle pulls a five-dollar bill out of his pocket. It's folded into a square, and he opens it before handing it over to the ponytailed guy behind the table. When the guy counts Kyle three ones back, Kyle folds them in half before tucking them away. That's when I realize that the folding is part of knowing what bills he's got. Amazing.

Meghan is giving Tessie a super rub along her smooth back, and the little dog closes her eyes slowly, blissed out. "Listen, Hayley," Meghan says, "do you have time to talk about the election?"

"What are you guys running for?"

"I'm running for vice president, and Meghan's running for president," I explain.

"Oh, against Omar," Kyle says.

"*What?*" Meghan screeches, and Tessie gives a little startled jump. "Sorry," Meghan tells the dog. "But —" She looks up at Kyle. "What?"

"Didn't you know that Omar is running?" Kyle asks.

"He's actually doing it?" Meghan is clearly still stunned.

"Wow," I say.

"Tell me that Jamil isn't running for veep," Meghan says.

"I don't think you're in danger there," Kyle admits. "Jamil isn't really interested in student government."

"Neither is Omar," Meghan snaps.

"Hmm," I say, and Kyle nods.

Meghan nibbles her gluten-free cookie. I wonder if she's still feeling lucky. "Okay," she says at last. "So, Hayley, now we *really* need to think election strategy, or else you'll end up working with Omar."

"This election is getting complicated," I say.

A look of horror crosses Meghan's face. "You're not dropping out, are you? You can't!"

"I won't, I won't," I promise. *Although I wish I could*, I think.

Kyle pops the lollipop into his mouth. "This is going to be interesting," he says.

That's the understatement of the year, I think.

Even though Kyle is blind, I get the feeling he sees things pretty clearly.

Confession:
*Stuff You Learn When
You Have a Dog*

1. A lot of people don't pick up their dog's poop. Not to be gross, but when you have a dog, they'll go and sniff anything that smells interesting. And, apparently, the most interesting smell in the world is poop. Having a dog means never just walking by someone's mess.

2. There are a lot of dogs in this world. The only thing dogs like to sniff more than poop is other dogs. When you actually have a dog, you meet them all.

3. People like to talk to dogs. When I walk down the street by myself, nobody says a word. When I'm with Tessie, everyone's like, "Hello, doggie!" and "Hi, dog!" and "Who's a good girl?" I don't bother pointing out that she

doesn't speak English, as it seems to make people so happy just to say hello.

4. Apparently, I drop a lot of food on the floor. Seriously, this dog is getting, like, eight meals a day.

5. You can tell a lot about people by the way they treat dogs. Like Meghan, for example, is a very enthusiastic petter. She gets Tessie riled up and excited. Kyle, on the other hand, approached Tessie slowly and patted her gently. She calmed down when she was with him. And that's how those guys are with everything. Meghan is all crazy energy, and Kyle is more tranquil. They're both fun . . . just in different ways.

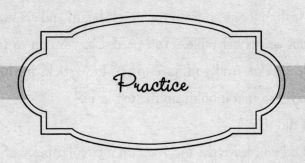

Practice

"This cake is deformed," I say to nobody in particular.

From across the counter, Chloe cocks her head. "It looks like Mount Tom."

"After an avalanche," Rupert adds in his quiet voice.

"Rupert!" Chloe protests, but I just laugh. He's right, after all. I'm standing behind the counter in the café, working on a wedding cake, but I've done something wrong. The top level is sinking into the bottom level, and it's a gigantic mess.

"I respect that you are still trying to frost that cake." Rupert's dark eyes are serious.

"Not for long." The frosting is only making everything worse. Besides, the cake is huge, and I can't reach the back of it.

Meghan looks up from the poster board and art supplies laid out across her table. "You need a lazy Susan to frost a wedding cake. And you have to put little sticks in the bottom layer so that it holds up the top layer."

"I did that!"

"Did you leave the top layer on a circular piece of cardboard?" Meghan asks.

"No."

"That's why it's sinking. The sticks are just poking holes in the bottom of the top layer. You need something solid to stop them." She goes back to coloring in her campaign poster.

"Grr! Why do you know these things?" I demand.

"Meh. My mom gets all of these cooking magazines," she explains. "I pick things up."

"I wish you wouldn't trouble yourself, dear," Gran says to me as she fills a fat white china teapot with hot water. "Why don't you just make a few cupcakes?" Her forehead is creased with worry as she eyes my wedding cake.

"Don't worry, Gran, I'll get it all worked out in time for your wedding," I tell her. "That's why I'm practicing."

"Well, it just seems like a lot of fuss, that's all. I don't think —"

"Well, now, my dear future Mrs. Malik!" Mr. Malik bustles into the café holding a sheaf of deep pink roses. "You're looking lovely."

"Oh, Umer." Gran's eyes brighten and she blushes as pink as the flowers. "Honestly! You'll go out of business bringing me flowers every day." But she doesn't refuse them. Instead, she takes the blooms and inhales deeply. "How lovely."

"If I go out of business, it will be thanks to that so-called restaurant next door to my flower shop!" Mr. Malik huffs as he perches on a stool by the counter. "They've vented the place improperly — it's making my whole store smell like a burrito!"

"Oh, dear!" Gran says. Chloe reaches for the flowers, and Gran hands them over, then pours Mr. Malik a cup of tea. I automatically reach for a madeleine — Mr. Malik's favorite — and place it on a plate.

"Thank you, my girls," he says. "A rose by any other name may smell as sweet, but a rose that smells like salsa is . . ."

"Un-Shakespearean," Rupert finishes.

"This is what happens when business owners aren't locals!" Mr. Malik grumbles.

"They aren't locals?" Chloe asks as she arranges Gran's roses in a vase.

"No, dear," Gran explains. "The restaurant is run by two businessmen in Boston."

Mr. Malik harrumphs. "It's really quite rude. But whenever I call to complain, I have to leave a message! I've complained to the manager, of course, a very nice lady, but she can't do anything about the vents without the owners' permission."

"Dreadful." Gran shakes her head. "Do have another madeleine, Umer."

"Mark my words — if they do this thing badly, they do everything else the same way," Mr. Malik pronounces. "I wouldn't eat at that restaurant for a million dollars."

That settled, Mr. Malik and my grandmother turn to discussing the news. My feet are starting to hurt from standing, so I give up frosting my monstrosity and head over to join Meghan at her table. "That looks good," I say, pointing to her poster.

"Artie gave me a few ideas."

"Really?" I think I mentioned that Artie and Meghan aren't exactly besties. "Well, it looks great."

Meghan leans back in her chair and stretches. She nods approvingly at the green-and-yellow posters. They really pop. "I've been doing this for over an hour," she says. "Want to take a walk?"

"Are you going for a walk?" Chloe asks, looking up from the book she just settled in to read. "Would you take Tessie? I'm just dying to finish this chapter."

"Sure!" Meghan says just as I let out a groan.

"You're doing the after-dinner walk," I tell Chloe. "And the one right before bedtime."

"No problem," she says, waving her hand at me.

Honestly, whatever happened to "I'll take care of the dog"? But, to tell the truth, I'm kind of glad that Chloe is sticking me with a bunch of the dog walking. That way, I can complain to Mom, and I know we won't get a permanent dog.

I'm very mean, I know.

I'm sorry.

But who likes picking up poop?

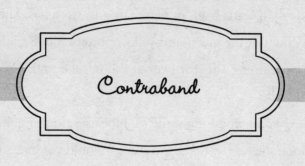

Contraband

"I can't believe how lucky you are!" Meghan chirps as she bounces down the street with my new-used lazy Susan. She's doing her bouncy-beach-ball walk. I don't even know how she does it, but it's like a little hop with each step. Like Tigger.

"You're even more excited about it than I am. Is it heavy?" Meghan insisted on carrying it, since I'm holding Tessie's leash.

"No — hardly anything. I just can't believe it! It was right there at a tag sale! It's, like, your Lazy Susan of Destiny! Look what Hayley got!" Meghan commands when she spots Marco walking toward us.

He snaps a photo of Meghan holding out the lazy Susan. "Cool," he says. "It's a plate."

"You can turn it," I explain to him. "It makes frosting cakes easier."

"Every home needs one," Marco jokes.

"Hayley found it at a tag sale for two dollars!" Meghan goes on. "Isn't that amazing? Isn't she lucky?"

"Yeah," Marco agrees. "Is that where you got the frog, too?"

"What frog?" I ask, and Marco points downward.

I look at the guilty-faced dog at the end of my leash. She is carrying a neon-green beanbag frog about the size of a lime. "Did you just shoplift that?" I ask Tessie, who just peers up at me with two neon-green legs sticking out of her mouth.

"She stole it from the tag sale! We're gonna get arrested!" Meghan cries.

Marco takes a photo of the dog with the frog. "Haven't you two been in trouble with the law before?" he asks.

"Don't remind me," I say, shooting a look at Meghan. The last time I was involved in a crime, Officer Ramon Martinez brought me home . . . and ended up dating my mom. Which turned out pretty well, actually. Except for the part where I got grounded. "We'll have to bring the frog back."

"They aren't going to take back a frog that has been slobbered on," Marco points out helpfully.

Ugh! Now I have to pay for Tessie's contraband? "I hope you're grateful," I say to the dog, who wags her tail at me. Oh, well. The tag sale is only charging twenty-five cents for small stuffed animals, so it won't exactly break the bank. Besides, it's partly my fault. I should have been watching her. I was just caught up in my lazy Susan purchase.

Marco snaps another photo, then looks at the camera screen. He laughs a little, then holds it out so I can see. He's managed to capture me frowning down at Tessie, and the little dog looking up at me adorably.

"Now there's a face that could get away with anything," Meghan says. She puts the lazy Susan on her hip and leans down awkwardly to give the dog a pat.

"Don't encourage her," I grumble as we fall into step back the way we came. Northampton sidewalks are pretty wide, and there are only a few stray singles and couples browsing the stores, so we have no trouble walking in a line together. Marco pauses to snap photos once or twice. He notices things I don't, like graffiti on a fire hydrant and a small patch of yellow crocuses blooming between the roots of an urban maple tree.

"Hey, Marco — do you have summer plans?" I ask.

"Not really," he says. "Why?"

"Well, there's this photography program at Islip Academy," I explain. "I think it's competitive to get in, but your stuff is so good —"

"You should do it!" Meghan chimes in. "My sister has a friend who did it last year and said it was amazing."

"I don't think my dad will go for it." Marco watches the usual snarl of pedestrians and cars in front of the converted department store that serves as Northampton's very own tiny mall. "It's probably expensive."

The faraway look on his face makes me sad. Marco's parents are . . . complicated. Well, *infuriating* might be a better word. Sometimes I wonder why they ever had children.

We reach the Unitarian Society, where a group of people have set things out on tables and blankets for a community tag sale. The scene of the crime.

"Listen, Hayley, I've got to run," Marco says suddenly, "but I've been thinking about the barbecue. Should I pick you up around seven thirty? I thought we should get there a little early, since I'm bringing the cooler and taking pictures and everything. You won't mind hanging out with me while I do that, right?"

Out of the corner of my eye, I catch sight of Meghan cocking her head and looking at me. I don't glance her way.

"Um, sure, Marco," I tell him. "That sounds great."

"Okay. Awesome." He clicks a picture of a bunch of old teapots at the tag sale, then heads down the street.

"So — uh — I think that blanket over there is where Tessie must have gotten the frog," I say, pointing to a small mountain of stuffed animals.

"Marco asked you to the barbecue?" Meghan asks.

That girl is extremely good at staying on target. "Um, yeah."

"When?"

"Uh — a couple of days ago?" *More like a week*, I realize.

"And yet you never mentioned it," Meghan points out. This is half observation, half question. What she's really asking is, *"Why?"*

"It just seemed like it wasn't a big deal." I tug Tessie's leash gently, and we start toward the cashier, where I explain the situation and hand over a quarter. The white-bearded Santa Claus–looking man who takes my money finds the whole situation uproarious, and then repeats the story about the shoplifting dog to a couple of women working nearby. Well, I'm glad that my foster dog's life of crime is amusing to someone.

This whole time, Meghan has been watching me with this Hmm look on her face.

"Stop looking at me," I tell her.

"Okay," she says.

We walk for a few moments.

"Stop thinking about me," I tell her.

Meghan laughs. "Okay, Hayley. You're right — it's not a big deal."

But we both know the truth: If I really didn't think it was a big deal, I would have mentioned it.

Confession:
I Love Marco

I love the way Marco can look at a crumpled piece of paper on the sidewalk and see something amazing.

I love the way he's so gentle with his sister, Sarah.

I love that he isn't afraid to stand up for what's right.

I love that he gave me his balloon in the first grade when mine soared away on a trip to the zoo.

I love that he always puts part of his allowance in the frog statue in front of the church downtown.

I love the far-off look he gets when he's thinking about something deep, like time, or stars.

I love that we've been friends since before we could walk, and that he knows me better than almost anyone.

I love that he thinks I'm amazing.

I love him like a brother. Even though he's handsome, and wonderful, and smart, and artistic. He kissed me, and I wondered if things could be different. But now I just don't think they can.

It doesn't make sense, but that's the way it is. I can't explain it, and I guess that's why I don't want to talk about it much.

"So I really need you to put that in the mail this week, William."

"Oh, sorry! I didn't realize you guys were on the phone. I'll just hang —"

"Hayley? No, that's okay. Your father and I were just wrapping up. I'll get off. Good-bye, William."

"Bye, Margaret. I'll take care of the dentist. Don't worry."

"Hi, Dad."

"Hey, Hayley! What are you doing Tuesday afternoon?"

"Um — I don't know. Homework, I guess."

"Wrong! You and I are heading out to Islip Academy for a tour and an interview! Isn't that great?"

"Oh. During school? Don't you have work?"

"I'm taking the afternoon off. I thought we could go out for dinner afterward or something."

"Okay, Dad."

"Just okay?"

"No — it sounds good."

"It's a beautiful campus. An incredible library — you'll love it. They even have stables!"

"For horses?"

"No, that's where the boarding students sleep. Of course for horses! You'll love it!"

"Sounds nice."

"It is. It's very nice."

"What should I wear?"

"Just be yourself, Hayley. Wear what you would normally wear. Maybe a skirt."

"I don't usu — Okay, Dad. I'll wear a skirt."

"I'll meet you in front of your school right at three, okay?"

"Great, Dad. Hold on, I'll get Chloe. Love you."

"Love you, too, Hayley! Trust me — this is going to be great!"

Pomelo Cupcakes

(makes approximately 12 cupcakes)

Pomelos are like Godzilla grapefruits. They're huge and have a thick skin. If you can't find one, a regular grapefruit will work, too. Delicious, unexpected, citrusy taste!

INGREDIENTS:

- 1-1/3 cups all-purpose flour
- 3/4 teaspoon baking powder
- 1/2 teaspoon baking soda
- 1/4 teaspoon salt
- 1/4 cup vanilla yogurt
- 3/4 cup granulated sugar
- 1/3 cup milk
- 1 teaspoon vanilla extract
- 1/4 cup pomelo juice
- 2 tablespoons finely grated pomelo zest
- 1/3 cup canola oil

INSTRUCTIONS:

1. Preheat the oven to 350°F. Line a muffin pan with cupcake liners.

2. In a large bowl, sift together the flour, baking powder, baking soda, and salt.

3. In a separate bowl, stir together the yogurt, sugar, milk, vanilla extract, pomelo juice and zest, and oil. With a whisk or handheld mixer, add the dry ingredients to the wet ones a little bit at a time, stopping to scrape the sides of the bowl a few times, and mix until no lumps remain.

4. Fill cupcake liners two-thirds of the way and bake for about 20–22 minutes. Transfer to a cooling rack, and let cool completely before frosting.

Pomelo Cream-Cheese Frosting

INGREDIENTS:

- 1/2 cup butter, softened
- 1/2 cup cream cheese, room temperature
- 4 cups confectioners' sugar
- 1/2 teaspoon vanilla extract
- 1/2 teaspoon lemon extract
- 2 teaspoons finely grated pomelo zest

INSTRUCTIONS:

1. In a large bowl, with an electric mixer, cream together the butter and cream cheese until they are fully combined and a lighter color, about 2–3 minutes.
2. Slowly beat in the confectioners' sugar in 1/2-cup batches, adding the vanilla extract, lemon extract, and pomelo zest toward the end.
3. Continue mixing the frosting on high speed for about 3–7 minutes, until the frosting is light and fluffy.

Bittersweet

"Um . . . what flavor is this again?" Artie asks as she dumps a half teaspoon of baking powder onto the mix of flour and sugar in the large white bowl.

"Grapefruit," I tell her.

She purses her lips in a way that says "cool" and "interesting" at the same time, only without words. I'm still getting used to having her here, in Gran's tiny kitchen, on a Saturday night. Game Night used to happen in my basement. That was back when I lived in a house, and Marco was my next-door neighbor, and Artie lived in the house behind ours. Back when our parents were friends.

Now our parents don't really talk anymore. And my friendships with Artie and Marco are all messed up. That's the thing that nobody tells you about some divorces — for a while, it can feel like nuclear fallout. Nothing survives.

And then, after a while, things start to grow back.

I guess that sounds depressing, but I don't really mean it that way. Things *do* grow back. And sometimes you even get a new species in the mix.

"Hey, hey, hey!" Meghan says as she walks into the kitchen. She stops up short when she sees Artie. "Oh! I just — I was just walking past the Tea Room, and your Gran said you were upstairs —"

"Hey, Meg. Artie and I are just making some cupcakes." I look at Artie, unsure how she'll react. She can be kind of possessive with her friends — she's one of those people who likes to have one-on-one time. But she's just mixing the batter and smiling, like it's no big deal.

"I didn't mean to interrupt," Meghan says.

"You're not interrupting," Artie tells her. "We were just about to put these in the oven and start a movie. Want to join?"

"Oh. Sure!" Meghan plops into a chair at the tiny table and watches as I use an ice cream scoop to fill the cupcake liners. "So — are these going to be for the barbecue?" she asks.

"Just a test run." My voice is a murmur . . . like I'm on tiptoe. Inwardly, I'm cringing. I don't want to talk about the barbecue in front of Artie.

"What time are you guys showing up for that?" Artie asks.

"I'll have to get there early to set up," Meghan says.

"I'll be there a little early, too," I put in.

"Okay. I hate being the first person to show up at a party," Artie says.

Meghan looks at me evenly, as if she's waiting for me to say something. I do not say, "Marco will be there, too." I don't want to get into it.

Meghan nods slowly, then looks over at Artie. Then back at me. "I think a few people will be there early, Artie. Don't worry." She drops her elbows onto the table and rests her chin on her palms. "So — what movie are we watching?"

"Well, I brought a few for us to choose from," Artie says. "Do you like Miyazaki?"

"Love him!" Meghan says. "Which ones have you got?"

"Back in a second, Hayley." Artie motions for Meghan to follow her, and they wander off toward the living room as I pull open the oven. Heat ruffles my hair as I put the tray of cupcakes on the top rack. Then I close the door with a clang and set the timer. I do all of these things without even realizing. They're automatic to me now.

Instead, all the time, I'm thinking about Artie, and how I missed my chance to tell her about Marco. I've missed it twice now.

I don't know how she'll react when she finds out, and I kind of can't deal with it. But she's going to find out, sooner or later. I can't keep putting it off.

I know I'm probably making things worse by not mentioning it, but I can't help it.

I just can't bear it.

I just. Can't.

In Training

"Sit. No, sit. Sit. Like this!" Chloe gets onto her knees to show Tessie how it's done.

"Now that hound is training you," Gran observes from her place at the dining table. It's Sunday night, and we're all scattered around the living and dining rooms. I'm lying on my stomach across the living room rug, decorating a HAYLEY HICKS FOR VICE PRESIDENT poster. Mom and Gran are sitting at the table in front of a messy pile of wedding magazines and brochures. And Chloe is trying to turn Tessie into a good dog with the help of a few Milk-Bones. Tessie hops around, eyeing the treat in Chloe's hand.

"I don't think she's getting it," I tell my little sister, who gets back to her feet.

"She's pondering her options," Chloe says, giving Tessie a treat.

"Now you've trained her to ignore you completely," I point out.

"But she's so cute! And she wants the treat! What am I supposed to do?"

"Forget a future career as a dog trainer." I go back to coloring in my name with a silver paint pen.

"Just wait," Chloe says. "I'll train her to carry the rings at Gran's wedding. Can I do that, Mom?"

Mom and Gran exchange a look, and Mom laughs. "No."

"Why not?" Chloe demands. "Everyone would love it!"

"Because you can't even train Tessie to stop eating the edge of your quilt," Mom says.

"Because I don't even care about that!" Chloe protests. "I think it's cute! It's not like Tessie can't be trained. She's house-trained, isn't she? And paper-trained! She could totally carry the rings down the aisle if we tied them to her collar with a ribbon!"

"Sweetheart, I don't even know if Tessie will be with us that long."

"She definitely won't," I say, and Chloe looks horrified.

"How can you say that?" Chloe wails, as if I've just won the Meanest Person on the Planet Award.

"Don't you want her to have a good permanent home?" I ask, and then I feel like a horrible sister because Chloe has tears in her eyes. "I mean . . . Chloe, we don't even know when Gran's wedding is going to be." I'm backtracking madly. "It could be a year from now!"

Chloe looks miserable, and clearly my mom thinks it's time to change the subject. "Mom," she says, turning to Gran, "Hayley's making a good point — do you have a date for the wedding?"

"Oh, not yet." Gran holds up her teacup and purses her lips at the rim. Then she places the cup in the exact center of the saucer.

"Well — I think you should decide soon. We can't really book a venue or caterer or anything until we have a date." Mom starts digging through the crazy pile and comes up with a brochure from Magic Hat Caterers. She frowns and flips it over. "Some of these people want a lot of lead time. How many guests were you thinking of having?"

"Oh, hmm. I hadn't given it much thought," Gran admits. "Perhaps just a few people. Something small."

"Does Mr. Malik have a big family?" I ask.

"Well, yes, quite large," Gran admits. "But I don't know if we'll invite them all."

"You don't want to offend anyone," Mom says. "Maybe you should talk it over with him. Get an idea of how many people you might like to have, then we can start looking at places. I love this one," she adds, pulling out a photo of a beautiful restaurant overlooking a waterfall. "That's about half an hour from here, but they can't take more than fifty people."

"Fifty? Rubbish," Gran says. "I don't need such an enormous wedding."

"Fifty is considered a small wedding," Mom says, handing the brochure to Gran, who takes it reluctantly. Mom starts making notes on a legal pad. "There are three of us. And Denise." Denise is my mom's sister. "And what about your sister and her children?"

"Granty Emily!" Chloe cheers. "And Edwin!"

"What about Josephine?" I ask, naming our other cousin.

"Meh," Chloe says with a shrug.

"And then there are definitely going to be some people from the groom's side," Mom puts in. "And you may even want to ask a few friends."

"Can Rupert come?" Chloe asks.

"Oh, honestly, this is all just so complicated," Gran huffs. "I think I'd rather cancel the wedding altogether and be done with it."

She takes a sip of her tea while we stare at her for a moment. Tessie even sits down. Finally.

Cancel the wedding? My blood feels thick as glue, my head like it's full of air. Not marry Mr. Malik? But that would be . . . That would be . . .

"You're joking, of course," Mom says, taking the brochure from Gran's hand. "Look, perhaps I'm giving you too much information. Why don't you sit down with Umer and talk it over? We can meet another time." Mom starts gathering the magazines into a tidy, colorful pile.

She's focused on making things orderly, but I can tell she's as upset as I am. Her face is pale, and she rakes her hair back in an anxious gesture I know well — I saw it a lot in the months after Dad moved out.

I'm so busy watching Mom and thinking that I don't even notice that Tessie has stepped onto my poster until a puddle makes its way toward my paint pen. "Chloe!" I screech. "What? Ohmigosh, Tessie! No! No!"

Tessie just looks up at my sister and keeps going until she is all out of pee.

"Gracious!" Gran exclaims as I shoo the dog off the poster. Mom dashes toward the kitchen for a roll of paper towels. "What has that animal been consuming?" Gran demands.

"So much for house-trained!" I growl at Chloe. "My poster is ruined!"

"She's paper-trained," Chloe protests. "If your paper is on the floor, she doesn't know the difference!"

Mom drops a pile of paper towels onto my poster, but it's not like it can be saved. I can't put up a poster covered in dog pee. Instead, I fold up the mess and carry it to the garbage. Then I spend about fifteen minutes washing my hands with antibacterial soap.

Mom comes up behind me and leans against the kitchen door frame. "Are you okay?" she asks gently.

No, I think. *No! I've got a poster covered in pee and Marco asked me to the dance and I don't want to go to another school and I don't think I even want to run for vice president and maybe Gran isn't getting married after all!* But I don't want to talk about any of it. "I can't wait until we get rid of that stupid dog," I snap exactly one split second before I realize that Chloe is standing right behind my mom.

My sister dashes off. A moment later, I hear the door to our room slam shut.

Mom and I look at each other for a moment.

"I should go after her," I say.

"Give yourself a few minutes," Mom says gently. "And give her a few. Do you want to talk?"

Here is a question: How do moms know when you're upset by more than just dog pee? "I want to think," I admit. "I'm going for a walk."

"Okay." Mom gives me a quick kiss on the forehead, and as her black curls tickle my face, I breathe in the familiar, comforting scent of her shampoo. I grab my coat from the hook and head out the back door. I don't want to have to explain everything to Gran.

I just want to go out into the twilight air and breathe awhile.

The Blues

$\mathcal{M}$y favorite store, Frantic, is two blocks up from the Tea Room. There are always really amazing window displays in the front and usually a street musician performing by the entrance. The store is packed with fun clothes, funny stuff, and beautiful room decorations. I usually can't afford to buy much, but it's the kind of store that's fun to look in, because there are a million things that make me smile.

Anyway, this week's window display is all shoes, and they've been set up so that they're walking in circles in this Dr. Seuss–style contraption. I'm not usually a shoe girl, but there's a pair of silver flats in the window that I really wish I could have. They sound dressy, but they aren't, and they look like they would be really comfortable. I have a pair of black flats, but they have a hole in the bottom near the toe on the right side, and the heels are worn down. I'm pretty hard on shoes. Anyway, I don't wear flats much. Just if I have someplace to go where I want to look nice. The problem is that my black flats are supposed to be my "nice" shoes, but they don't look nice at all. I could use some new ones. But since I don't really go to that many nice places, I really don't want to ask Mom for the money. It seems kind of dumb. So, instead, I just watch those pretty silver shoes pad around in a circle with the other shoes in the display, back and forth, back and forth.

I'm debating whether or not to go inside and try on a pair — just for informational purposes — when I hear a familiar voice nearby.

"Hey, that was great," Kyle says to the guitarist sitting on the curb. "Do you know anything by Muddy Waters?"

"Do I know any Muddy?" The guitarist breaks into a grin and busts into a blues riff. Then he starts singing in a deep, gravelly voice. He's football-shaped, with large glasses and a heavy beard, and he holds his guitar like he's about to wrestle it to the ground. I've seen him playing on the street a few times, but I've never stopped to listen before.

Kyle is nodding and tapping his foot to the beat. He claps once or twice, like he wishes he had something to do with his hands. I imagine that if there were a piano nearby, he would hop onto the bench and join in.

I go stand beside him, and when the song is over, I say, "Hey, Kyle, it's me — Hayley!"

"Fred!" Kyle is beaming, as if my presence has just put a cherry on top of the best day ever. "Do you know Winthrop Little?"

Winthrop tips his hat, revealing long, scraggly gray hair, and I giggle a little as I say hello. For one thing, the guy looks more like a renegade motorcyclist than a "Winthrop." For another, he's definitely not "little."

"Pleased to meet you," Winthrop says politely.

"Winthrop loves jazz," Kyle says. "We like all the same records."

"Really, I'm a blues man." Winthrop strums a few bluesy chords.

"He's played all over the country," Kyle tells me. "Even opened for some of the greats."

"All true," Winthrop puts in.

"Wow." I want to ask Winthrop what he's doing in Northampton, but I don't want to be rude. Mostly, I just think it's amazing that I've seen him on the street maybe fifty times, and I've never really listened to him before.

"Listen, I've got to get going," Kyle says, digging in his pocket. He drops a folded bill into Winthrop's open guitar case. "Catch you later."

"On the flip," Winthrop says. "See you around, Hayley." Then he launches into a new song.

Winthrop's deep, bluesy voice follows us as Kyle and I fall into step down the street. "So — what's up, Hayley?" Kyle asks.

"Oh, nothing."

"You seem . . . thoughtful." Kyle doesn't say more. He's not the type to ask questions.

"I just . . . I kind of yelled at Chloe for something that really isn't her fault." I explain about Tessie and the poster.

"Aww — you yelled at two puppies, huh?"

"Kind of," I admit.

Kyle nudges me gently on the shoulder. "It's okay, Hayley. Chloe knows you love her. People get mad sometimes; it's no big deal. And dogs never hold a grudge."

"That's the truth." I stop walking and inhale a deep lung-ful of cold spring air. It's misty, and a little cold, but I don't mind. I can feel the damp on the tips of my eyelashes.

"Hayley — are you going to the barbecue?" Kyle asks suddenly. "I was wondering if you might want to go together?"

The dampness on the ends of my eyelashes thickens, and Kyle blurs in front of me. My throat is closing, and I feel like I'm going to choke.

Kyle waits a moment, and then flashes an embarrassed smile. "You aren't saying anything," he says. "Are you — thinking it over?"

"Kyle, I —" There is a lot that I wish I could say, but don't really dare. "Marco asked me already." My words are limp, but they're the best I can do.

"Oh. So you're going with him."

"I've already said yes."

"Got it." Kyle looks like he understands. Like maybe he understands the whole thing.

Like maybe he understands it better than I do.

And who knows? Maybe he does.

Confession:
Five-Dollar Bill

Kyle dropped a five-dollar bill into Winthrop's guitar case. It was folded in a square. I saw it.

And I know Kyle did that on purpose. He isn't one of the rich kids. Or he doesn't seem to be. But how many kids in my school would have given five dollars to a street musician? How many would stop to talk to him?

When I'm with Kyle, the world just seems bigger, somehow. More interesting. Brighter. It seems like an adventure, and anyone who is brave enough is welcome to step into it.

It's like he sees the best in people. I know he sees the best in me. When I'm around him, I just wish that I could be more like him.

He's so easy to talk to. You never have to make anything up.

And here is the real confession:

I wish I could say yes.

Yes!

Yes!

Poster

"Amazing job, Artie. As usual," Meghan says as she stands back from the lime-and-yellow poster. It really pops against the bland beige wall.

"Thanks!" Artie grins as she makes a minuscule adjustment to make it even straighter than it was before.

"What was wrong with the old posters?" I ask.

Meghan jumps a little and turns to face me. "Oh, hi, Hayley. I didn't realize you were there. Studies show that people stop seeing the posters after a few days or so. It's good to freshen them up. We'll surprise everyone tomorrow morning." The last bell rang ten minutes ago, and the halls are deserted. I'm only here this late because I have to talk to Señor Derby about the advanced class situation.

"But we're keeping everything in the same color palette," Artie explained, waving the old yellow poster. "So that people recognize the brand."

"Great," I say, as if I know what we're talking about.

"You should do your posters in green and yellow, too," Artie suggests, "so that people realize that you two are together."

"Brilliant!" Meghan says, holding her hand up for a high five. Then Artie says, "Thank you" in a British accent, and Meghan says, "No, thank you" in the same accent, and they go on that way for a while, and all the time I'm just standing there, like, "Say whaa?" Because — since when do those two have an in-joke?

"Okay," I tell them. "I have to start over with my posters, anyway." I explain about the dog pee incident.

"Yeah, Meghan and I have been meaning to ask you why your posters weren't up yet," Artie says. "We were wondering."

"If you need help, just let us know," Meghan says, and now I'm seriously feeling weird, because since when do Artie and Meghan get together to talk about *me*?

"Uh — I'll try to get them up tomorrow," I tell them, even though I'm a little annoyed that I'm not getting any sympathy for the dog situation.

"Well, well, well," Omar says as he rounds the corner. "I see you've finally managed to organize something, Meghan."

"I've been organizing stuff all year, Omar," she snaps.

Omar just purses his lips as he holds up his campaign poster and rips a piece of tape from a roll with his teeth. Then he slaps up the tape — not even straight along the edges, just all wonky and haphazard — and plasters the poster right next to Meghan's. Omar's poster isn't as pretty as Meghan's. At all. It's just large, chunky black lettering written crooked on the right. But what it lacks in prettiness, it makes up for in largeness. It's huge.

Meghan takes one look at it, and I practically see steam coming out of her ears. " 'Ideas that matter'?" she demands, reading the poster.

"Yeah — good one, right?" Omar says.

"Like my ideas don't matter?"

"I didn't realize you had any ideas," Omar replies.

"Omar!" I say. "That's not fair. Meghan's done a lot of stuff."

"I have a ton of ideas," Meghan huffs. "Just because I didn't like your one idea —"

Omar glares at her. "Meghan, the role of the class president is to listen to the people in the class, then help them make things happen."

"Omar — the class president has to do one thing at a time," Meghan says. Her voice sounds strained, like it's taking her a lot of effort not to start screeching. "You couldn't lead a trip to the bathroom."

"I guess we'll let the class decide," he says, and turns on his heel to walk away.

Artie shakes her head, frowning at the poster. "Unreal. He didn't even hang it up straight."

"Don't you dare," I say as Meghan reaches for the poster.

"What?" She looks guilty as she pulls the poster off the wall. "I'm just straightening it." She hangs it up again, although I'm pretty sure she wanted to shove it in the trash. She stares at it a moment longer, then sighs. "Okay. I can't let this get to me."

"It isn't personal," Artie tells her.

"Well — it kind of *is* personal," Meghan says. "But that doesn't mean I have to care. I'll be a better president than Omar, no matter what he thinks. And besides — I have other stuff to think about. Like the barbecue. Speaking of —"

"We were going to get some frozen yogurt and talk about decorations," Artie announces. "Do you want to come?"

The mention of the barbecue has made me feel slightly queasy. "No, I — no, thanks. I have to meet Señor Derby."

"Oh, I was thinking," Artie went on, "since I'll have to do decorations, and Hayley is making cupcakes, and Meghan is in charge of the whole thing, maybe we should meet up early and all go over to the barbecue together?"

Meghan lifts her eyebrows at me, but she doesn't say anything.

I think about the moments that I've already let pass by — the moments in which I could have told Artie about Marco. But this isn't like those moments. If I let this one pass, it's as good as a lie. I have to say something. "Uh . . . I think I'm already going with Marco."

"Well, whatever. He can join," Artie says.

I look over at Meghan, my face pleading.

"I don't think it's that kind of situation." Meghan's voice is gentle.

Artie looks at Meghan for a long moment, as if it's taking time for this sentence to compute. Finally, Artie looks at me. "Oh," she says.

I want to say that I don't know what kind of situation it is, but I know that will only make things messier. Instead, I inspect a crack in the floor that I'd never noticed before. It looks a little like the northern border of Texas. How fascinating.

"Okay, well . . . Okay." Artie tosses her gorgeous long hair over her shoulder, and smiles as if this is all normal — fine — just what she expected, although I'm sure it isn't. "Are you ready to get going, Meghan?"

"Sure," Meghan says. "See you later, Hayley." She gives me a little hug, and then heads down the hall.

Artie doesn't say good-bye. She just follows Meghan out the door.

Confession:
Weirdness

It's not that I'm jealous, or possessive. I'm not like that.

It's just weird to think that maybe Artie and Meghan are eating frozen yogurt and talking about me.

Maybe Artie is telling Meghan all about the time she confessed to me that she had a crush on Marco. Maybe she's telling Meghan that she saw me kissing Marco just a few weeks later.

Maybe Meghan is thinking that it's strange that I never told her about the kiss.

Maybe Meghan is thinking that we aren't good friends after all.

Maybe Meghan is thinking that she likes Artie better than she likes me.

Maybe Artie is coming up with all kinds of great ideas for the barbecue.

Maybe she's working on more fabulous posters for Meghan right now.

I imagine them wondering, "Why are we even friends with Hayley, anyway?"

And Artie says, "She can't even get her posters done."

And Meghan says, "Maybe you should run for vice president, Artie."

I imagine them tasting each other's frozen yogurt and laughing, and talking about making each other friendship bracelets and planning sleepovers and stuff.

But that probably isn't happening, right?

It definitely isn't.

Except that they were going to talk to me about my posters.

So who knows?

It's not that I don't want my friends to be friends with each other. Well, it's not exactly like that. Maybe it's a little like that.

I just want them both to like me best.

Is that wrong?

Pistachio Cupcakes

(makes approximately 12 cupcakes)

I love pistachios! These cupcakes aren't green, but they're packed with pistachio flavor.

INGREDIENTS:

- 1 cup plus 2 tablespoons all-purpose flour
- 1/2 cup ground toasted pistachios
- 1 teaspoon baking powder
- 1/2 teaspoon baking soda
- 1 tablespoon ground flaxseeds
- 1/2 teaspoon salt
- 3/4 cup granulated sugar
- 2/3 cup milk
- 1 teaspoon vanilla extract
- 1/3 cup canola oil

INSTRUCTIONS:

1. Preheat the oven to 350°F. Line a muffin pan with cupcake liners.

2. In a large bowl, sift together the flour, ground pistachios, baking powder, baking soda, ground flaxseeds, and salt.

3. In a smaller bowl, stir together the sugar, milk, vanilla extract, and oil. Using a whisk or a handheld mixer, add the wet ingredients to the dry ones a little bit at a time, stopping to scrape the sides of the bowl a few times, and mix until no lumps remain.

4. Fill cupcake liners two-thirds of the way and bake for 20–22 minutes. Transfer to a cooling rack, and allow to cool completely before frosting.

Pistachio Buttercream Frosting

INGREDIENTS:

- 1 cup butter, softened
- 3-1/2 cups confectioners' sugar
- 1–2 tablespoons milk
- 1-1/2 teaspoons vanilla extract
- 2–3 tablespoons ground toasted pistachios

INSTRUCTIONS:

1. In a large bowl, with an electric mixer, cream the butter until light in color, about 2–3 minutes.
2. Slowly beat in the confectioners' sugar in 1/2-cup batches, adding a little bit of milk whenever the frosting becomes too thick.
3. When all the confectioners' sugar has been combined, add the vanilla extract and ground pistachios, and continue mixing on high speed for about 3–7 minutes, until the frosting is light and fluffy.

Questions

"So? So?" Dad puts down the magazine he was idly flipping through and stands up. Annie looks up from the e-reader she brought with her. "How did it go?" Dad asks.

"Take it down a notch," I murmur, then turn to wave at the Islip admissions officer who just interviewed me. I wave at Ms. Stoneham, and she waves back.

"Thanks so much for coming in, Hayley." She smiles at my dad. "It was so nice meeting you, Mr. Hicks and Ms. Montri." This woman is built like a stick bug — all bony arms and legs. She's wearing a dowdy skirt and a pink sweater set, but somehow looks elegant, anyway.

"I know Hayley will be very happy here," Dad says.

I resist the urge to roll my eyes and say, "Dad!" Instead, I just smile and smile until my face aches.

"Is it all right if we look around the campus?" Annie asks.

"Yes! In fact, I encourage it. There's a small café in the library, if you'd like an espresso or latte, and it's a very pleasant walk to the other end of campus. Do you have a map?" Ms. Stoneham pulls one from a display on the wooden coffee table at the center of the room.

I take it, even though I already have a map somewhere in my book bag. My dad makes small talk for another few minutes, and then we head out into the light drizzle.

"So, how did it go?" Dad asks once the door to the admissions building has closed behind us.

"I don't really know. Well, I think." I'm pretty sure Ms. Stoneham liked me. She smiled at my report card and laughed twice during the interview. But I'd never had an interview before, so I wasn't really sure what they were supposed to be like. Maybe laughing is bad.

The campus is made up of several classical brick buildings, and you would think that it might look dreary on a gray day. But the light rain is actually making the lawns look brilliant green. "It's so beautiful here," I say.

"Isn't it?" Annie agrees. "Wow. Can you imagine going to school here? My school back in Thailand was a single building! And not even a very big one."

"Hayley's current school looks more like an old mental institution," Dad says.

"Dad!"

"Sorry. But it's that old giant prison style. . . ."

I shake my head. What he's saying is true. But still. I like my school, even if it's kind of ugly. I mean, it can't help being ugly.

A knot of girls in pastel denim skirts and pretty sweaters heads toward us. Two of them have brightly patterned umbrellas, and the third has a black one with a lining that looks like a blue sky dotted with white clouds. Those umbrellas reek of expense, and I can't help glancing up at my somewhat lopsided red one, which is coming off the spoke in one place.

One of the girls — the one with long, glossy black hair — smiles at me as they all three keep walking down the path toward the arts building. Yes, they have a whole building for the arts. That's just the visual arts, by the way: painting, sculpture, photography, and so on. Dance and theater have a separate building. So does music.

"That girl is carrying a Marc Jacobs bag." Annie sounds shocked.

"Is that —" My dad shakes his head. "What is that? Is that good?"

"It's *expensive*," Annie says.

"Even I've heard of it," I say, to give Dad some idea. He knows I have zero clue when it comes to clothing brands.

"My parents never would have let me have a bag like that when I was a teenager," Annie says. "Not even if they were zillionaires. Which they were *not*," she adds quickly.

"So . . . it's bad?" Dad seriously doesn't know what to make of it.

Annie and I exchange a glance. "It is what it is," I say to Dad. But I know what Annie is getting at. These people *are* zillionaires. At least, they dress like it. And they — I don't know — they walk like it. They have umbrellas like it.

The truth is, I'm feeling a little shabby.

I can't really picture myself at Islip Academy. Mostly because I can't picture someone in jeans with pistachio cupcake batter on her sweatshirt roaming across these perfect green lawns. And I can't see myself wearing a skirt and a button-down shirt for a regular old school day, like the girls we just passed.

I'm too busy wondering how those girls manage to have gleamy hair and glowy skin to notice the puddle in front of me, so I step in it. "Ugh!"

"What's wrong?" Dad asks.

"Oh — the water just sloshed through the hole in my shoe," I admit. Now my shoes are squish, squish, squishing and my toes are cold.

"Why don't we get you some new shoes?" Dad suggests.

"Well — I don't wear fancy shoes much," I admit.

Dad is looking at me with his head cocked to the side. It's the same look Tessie gives when she's trying to figure out what we mean when we say "sit." It's like, "*Yo no comprendo.*" "Does it make sense to have nice shoes with a hole in the bottom?" Dad asks.

"Uh, no." I feel a blush creep to my cheeks.

"Let's go downtown and get the shoes," Annie says. "Then we can go out to dinner."

I have to laugh a little. Annie's always up for shopping.

"Well, there is a pair that I saw at Frantic," I admit.

"So, let's get them!" Dad crows. "Once we're finished poking around the library."

"Sounds good to me," Annie says, and I hesitate a moment, then nod.

I may never be a rich girl, and I may never fit in at Islip, but I can have the right shoes. And I guess that's better than nothing.

From the Phone Files:
Part 2

"Hayley? It's Meg."

"Oh. Hey! What's up?"

"Meh. Campaign insanity and barbecue awkwardness."

"Yeah . . ."

"That Artie moment was pretty painful."

"Don't talk about it."

"Okay . . . What's the story there? Does she like Marco or something?"

"Is this not talking about it?"

"Sorry. Sorry. But — can I ask one question?"

"If I say no, will you ask it anyway?"

"Why don't you like Marco? He's a nice guy. I mean, he has a temper, but he's sweet. And cuh-yoot! Those eyes! I mean — you know, you've been friends for such a long time. Maybe it makes sense to try something else."

"Meghan! It isn't like that! I can't like someone just because I, like, should."

"Hmm."

"It doesn't make sense, I guess."

"No. It does. I mean, I had that crush on Ben Habib, even though it was hopeless, right? Besides, maybe you like someone else better . . . If you know what I'm saying . . . Hello? Are you still there?"

"Yeah."

"You like Kyle, right?"

"What? No."

"Hmm."

"Whatever. Maybe. I don't know!"

"It's okay."

"Look — I don't even know. Do you think that he thinks I do?"

"I have no idea."

"He asked me to the barbecue."

"Ooooh."

"What do you mean, 'Ooooh'?"

"I mean that I'm putting some stuff together in my mind. Like, Kyle asked you to the barbecue, but you'd already said yes to Marco, and so you had to say no. And weirdness ensued. No wonder you've been acting . . ."

"What? What? How have I been acting?"

"I don't know. However you've been acting. Like, full of thought? Even Artie was like, 'What's up with Hayley, she hasn't done her posters.' Anyway, I get it now."

"Okay."

"Are you mad? Don't be mad."

"I'm just — okay. I'm not mad."

"Good."

"Meg —"

"Yeah?"

"Do you ever wish we were back in third grade? Like — do you ever wish we didn't have to think about crushes and barbecues and all of that stuff?"

"No. I like planning barbecues. Obviously. Why — do you?"

"Sometimes. I guess I just wish things were simple."

"Were things simple in the third grade? That's not how I remember it. Are things simple for Chloe?"

"Not exactly. You've got a point, Meghan."

"I usually do. Somewhere in there. Listen, I've got to go. My mom is screaming that I have to tell her what I want in my lunches for the rest of the week or I'm getting nothing but Tofurky sandwiches on gluten-free bread."

"Is that a threat?"

"Whatever — it's working. I'll see you at school, okay?"

"Sure, Meg. Bye."

"Bye, Hayley."

Silly Puppy

"Fetch! Go get it, Tessie! Go on!" Chloe gestures down the hall, where she has just tossed Tessie's favorite stuffed animal — which is actually a stuffed vegetable. It's a fuzzy carrot. "Go get it!"

Tessie cocks her head, like a parrot getting ready to squawk.

"Go get it, girl!"

"She doesn't understand why you just threw her toy away," Rupert interprets.

"I didn't throw it away — I want her to fetch it! Ugh!" Chloe stomps toward the carrot, but Tessie — sensing that Chloe is about to grab her beloved toy again — races in front of her and snatches up the carrot. "Drop it! Drop it, girl!"

"She isn't dropping it," Rupert says as Tessie races back into our tiny living room and scrambles to the other side of the coffee table.

"Get that stuffie!" Chloe commands.

My legs are tucked under the table, and I am happy to take a break from conjugating irregular verbs. "Here — let me have the carrot, Tessie." I lean over to try to grab the toy, but Tessie hops away from me. It's a pretty good trick, since the carrot is almost the same size as her entire body.

"Get the carrot, Rupert!" Chloe shouts.

Rupert looks at her with his eyebrows lifted over the top of his glasses.

"Sorry." My sister blushes. "I just got carried away." She dives for Tessie, and the dog streaks under the table. Rupert tries to stop her, but his knee knocks against the table, spilling my tall glass of iced tea all over my homework.

"Chloe!" I shout.

"Oh, sorry, sorry!" Chloe tries to herd Tessie out of the way, but the little dog is already trotting off — still holding the giant fuzzy carrot — to her bed in the corner.

Rupert dashes to the kitchen and comes back with a bunch of paper towels.

"What's going on in here?" Mom asks as she walks through the door holding a paper bag full of groceries. Chloe takes the towels from Rupert and starts trying to dry my homework, but the ink has run all over the page. "Homework catastrophe," I say. "I'm going to have to start all over."

"Chloe?" Mom turns to my sister.

"I was just trying to teach Tessie to fetch," Chloe wails.

"Next time, outside," Mom says. "Are you okay, Hayley?"

I shoot a glare at Tessie, who is curled around her carrot and looking at me with guilty eyes. I'm super irritated with that dog. I'm about to say so when I look over at Chloe, whose eyes are filled with tears. Kyle's words, *Yelled at two puppies, huh?* come back to me, and I sigh. "Yeah, it's — it's no big deal. I can still read most of what I wrote. I'll just copy it over."

Mom nods. "Chloe, at least get Hayley another glass of water."

"Okay!" Chloe darts toward the kitchen, clearly glad to have something to do.

"It was iced tea!" I call after her.

"I'll tell her," Rupert says, and hurries after my sister.

"Thanks, Hayley," Mom says, balancing the bag of groceries on the living room table.

"What for?"

Mom sits down in one of the chairs. "Just . . . for not yelling at the dog. I know you wanted to." She smiles a little, then catches sight of my feet, sticking out on the other side of the coffee table. "Have I seen those shoes before?"

"Uh — no."

Our eyes meet for a moment, and I feel my ears getting hot.

"Dad got them for you?" Mom says.

"Yes."

"They're nice."

The air feels full of things she isn't saying, and I feel them falling on me, like rain. I wonder if my father ever paid his half of the textbook. I wonder if he paid the dental bill. I wonder how I could possibly ask, and I know that I can't.

Chloe and Rupert come back into the living room. "I put one teaspoon of sugar in it, just how you like it," Chloe announces.

"And I got out the ice cubes," Rupert adds as she places the glass on the table, in just the same spot where the old one was.

I can't help laughing a bit at how earnest they are. "Great," I say. "Perfect, thank you."

Chloe crosses the room and kneels down beside Tessie. She strokes the dog's head gently. "And I'm sorry I chased you around the room," she says gently. "I just wanted you to fetch your carrot." She puts her cheek to Tessie's head, and the little dog licks her face.

"Dinner in half an hour," Mom announces, picking up the grocery bag and heading into the kitchen. "Chloe, you're on table setting. Hayley, you're on dishes. Gran's at her bridge club, so she'll be home late."

Chloe is still nuzzling Tessie and whispering into her floppy little ears. Rupert sits beside Chloe, gently stroking Tessie's back.

I get back to work on my Spanish, wondering how people can be so wonderful and cause such problems at the same time.

Project: Landslide

"Brilliant! Brilliant! Brilliant!" Meghan crows as she flings open the door to the café. Everyone turns to look at her. "Go on about your business!" she announces in a general way as she waves at the customers. Artie is trailing in her wake, holding rolled-up poster board.

"What's up?" I ask as they plop themselves onto stools in front of the counter.

"Project: Landslide!" Meghan announces.

"I see Hayley's already working on it," Artie puts in, and both of them giggle. She's referring to my latest wedding cake attempt. It has some . . . challenges.

I sigh, and Artie apologizes. "I'm sorry — I shouldn't

have said that," she says. "It's just — your cupcakes are always so pretty."

"You can't have cupcakes at a wedding," I say.

"Why not?" Meghan demands. "I'm going to have chocolate-chip cookies!"

"You would." Artie rolls her eyes. A few weeks ago, a comment like that would have had Artie and Meghan at each others' throats, but now they just look at each other and giggle.

I put down my frosting bag and wipe my hands on a tea towel. "So — what's Project: Landslide?"

"Our guaranteed election-winning platform," Meghan explains. "Omar wants ideas? I'll show him ideas! I've got everything all planned, and I'm going to announce it all when I give my election speech. When I am president — ahem" — Meghan grins — "I plan to hold a Green Up day to beautify our school, a book drive, and a food drive for the shelter."

"Plus two dances and a bowling night!" Artie gushes. They high-five.

"Sounds fun," I say.

"You bet it does," Meghan agrees. "Plus — meaningful stuff for the do-gooderish types!"

"Um, so who's going to organize all of this?" I ask.

"We are!" Meghan chirps. "Who else? The prez and veep!"

"Um . . . it sounds like a lot of work," I point out.

"No, no — it'll be fun!" She holds up her hand, scout style. "Swearsies!"

I cast a glance around the café, wondering if I'll still have time to work here if I win vice president. I really love helping out Gran at the café. I'd hate to give it up.

And then there's my dad. He's foaming at the mouth for me to go to Islip. He's even arranged for me to sit in on a class there in a couple of days. Mom isn't so sure, but she says it all depends on scholarship money. Which means that she isn't saying no.

I don't mention that, though. What's the point of freaking Meghan out? I mean, I may not end up at Islip Academy. I probably won't. Like, 30 percent chance I will. I think.

"Do you really think we can pull all that off?" My voice sounds doubtful, even to me.

"We'll just rope in a bunch of people to help," Meghan promises. "Like Artie."

"I'll totally help," Artie says.

"Why don't you run for vice president?" The words are out of my mouth before I have a chance to think about how they'll sound to Meghan, who gasps.

"It's a little late," Artie says. "Besides, I can't stand the idea of running for something. What if I don't get elected?"

"You're not backing out, are you?" Meghan's blue eyes are wide with horror. "Hayley, you can't leave me hanging!"

"No, no," I say quickly. "Of course not!" Inside, I cringe. "This sounds like a great plan for the year," I add truthfully. It does sound like a great plan.

And if someone else were doing it, I'd be really super excited about it.

Okay, I tell myself. *Okay. We'll get help. We'll manage it.* This silent pep talk is for myself, as Artie and Meghan have already started talking about the Green Up day, and making notes on Meghan's clipboard pad.

"Hayley?" Mom calls from the rear office. "Could you come back here, please?"

I hurry to the back room, and Mom holds up a red sweater with a very mangled sleeve. "Did you borrow my sweater without asking?"

"Mom — are you serious?" I ask. Okay, the truth is that

I did once borrow a sweater without asking. But it wasn't her good red cashmere sweater. Besides, if I borrowed a sweater, I might spill something on it, but I wouldn't *chew* it. "I have a prime suspect," I tell her. "And she's covered in fur."

Mom looks at the sweater again, and notices the telltale dog hair. "I shouldn't have left it out on my bed," she says.

"Just like I shouldn't have left my poster out on the floor."

Mom glances at the door that leads to the back apartment stairs. "I should have known we couldn't handle a dog."

"We don't know what we're doing," I point out. "Maybe if we knew how to train her . . ." My voice trails off.

Mom shakes her head at the ruined sweater. It's the nicest top she has, and it always looks really great with her dark, curly hair.

Rest in peace, sweater, I think. *You'll be missed.*

"Chloe will be heartbroken," Mom says. It's like she's talking to the sweater.

"Mom — we were just supposed to foster Tessie," I remind her. "We were never going to keep her."

Mom looks uncomfortable, and I wonder if she and Chloe have been having some conversations I don't know about.

"We really can't keep her," Mom says.

"We really can't," I agree.

"Okay," Mom says.

"Okay."

She nods, and I head back out into the café. I pause beside the glass display case for a moment, watching Artie laugh as Meghan jots something down. I have a horrible dropping-off-a-cliff feeling in my stomach, and I'm trying hard to figure out why.

Is it because I know Chloe will be disappointed about Tessie?

Is it because I don't really want to be vice president?

Is it because I might have to stop working at the café?

Is it because I might have to go to Islip Academy?

Is it because Meghan and Artie seem to like each other better than they like me right now?

Is it because Marco asked me to the barbecue?

Is it because Kyle did?

Or is it all of the above?

Out at Islip

"Hey — were you just sitting in?" a girl with the short black hair asks me. "I'm Rachel — what did you think of the class?" Her blue eyes are huge, and her pale skin makes her look like a mod Snow White.

"I thought it was great," I admit. "It's cool that you read novels in history class. I'm Hayley, by the way."

"Great to meet you. Yeah, Mr. Denning is really into era-appropriate lit," Rachel says. "He says it gives us a 'feel for the values of the age.' Last semester was the Ancient Greeks, and we went through the *Iliad* and the *Odyssey*. Are you going to look in on anything else?"

"I thought that was the last class of the day," I tell her.

"It was — but the studios have drop-in time." Rachel nods toward the arts building. "Come with me, if you want. Then you can check out some of the extracurriculars."

"I wish I'd thought of that," I say as we fall into step. "But I told my dad to pick me up at three."

Rachel laughs. "Just text him and ask him to come later."

"I don't have a cell phone," I admit.

"Oh!" She looks really surprised. "Oh — do you want to borrow mine?"

"No, that's okay. Thanks."

Rachel shrugs and pulls open the door and holds it for me. Someone is coming out just as I start in, and I run right into Marco. He stares for a moment, then breaks into a smile. "Hey," he says.

"Oh — hi!" I introduce Rachel, then say, "What are you doing here, Marco?"

He gives me a heavy-lidded look. "Someone sent my mom a bunch of information about Islip Academy's summer photography program," he says. "You don't have any idea who might have done that, do you?"

"No," I say.

He looks like he doesn't believe me, but it's completely true. I didn't send it.

"You should definitely do it, if you can," Rachel says. "All the summer programs are great. I know a lot of people can't work it in, with trips and camp and stuff, but if you have the time . . ."

Marco gives me this little smile. We both know that his family isn't going on any fancy trips. And they aren't sending him to camp, either. It's funny how "If you have the money" doesn't seem to have entered Rachel's brain. She reminds me of my dad a little, and I wonder if all the kids at Islip are like that.

Marco casts a glance across the rolling green lawns. You know that expression "The grass is always greener on the other side of the fence"? Let me tell you, up here, it's literally true. At my school, the grass in front is patchy with mud and bare spots. Here, the only patches come from daffodils that have started springing up at the edges of the perfect lawns. I know it sounds crazy, but the weather seems better here, too. I swear that when I left home this morning, the sky was half clouds. But now, it's blue out to the horizon.

"Listen, I've got to get going," Rachel says. "Nice meeting you, Hayley and Marco. Hope I see you around."

Marco and I say good-bye to Rachel and start back toward the main building. "This place is seriously nice," Marco says.

"True," I admit.

"Maybe a little too nice."

"Is that even possible?" I ask, but even as I say it, I know what Marco means. It *is* a little too nice. A little too manicured. The people are a little too rich.

"Would I be crazy to go here?" Marco asks. "Or crazy not to?"

He says this quietly, like he's asking himself, not me. So I don't answer.

I'm not sure I know the answer, anyway.

Poster Girl

"Hayley?"

The voice at my elbow is gentle, and it takes me a moment to recognize it. "Artie — hi."

"Hi." She glances quickly over her shoulder, then faces me and smiles. "Um, hey, I just wanted — I notice your posters aren't up yet. For vice president." She twirls her hair as she says this, as if she's afraid to bring up the subject.

"Yeah, I know — sorry. I just haven't had time. Things have been crazy ever since —"

"No big deal — it's just time is running out."

"I know, I know."

"And Anthony's had his posters up for a week —"

"Right, I know."

Anthony Adams is running for vice president, too. Meghan doesn't think he's likely to win, since he's always talking about how great he is and nobody can stand it, but still. I should at least let people know that they have another choice.

"I hope this isn't awkward, but I kind of —" Artie shrugs and unrolls a large yellow poster with green lettering.

Hayley Hicks for Eighth-Grade Veep! Pretty Sweet.

"Oh, thanks," I say. She has outlined the letters in silver glitter and painted a glittery cupcake in the corner. It's really pretty, and very me. And it even coordinates with Meghan's posters. "That's really . . . great."

Artie studies my face. "Are you mad?"

"Totally not."

"I should've let you do it."

"No — seriously. Thank you! I love it."

"I made three of them."

"Wow." I take the posters from her. She slings her backpack

forward and pulls out a roll of green painter's tape. "You're an excellent campaign manager."

"Well, I . . . I guess I just think you'll be a really great vice president. You're, like — you're like the string on Meghan's balloon."

I laugh a little at the image. "Tying her down?"

"More like keeping her from floating away. I mean —" She looks over her shoulder again, as if she hopes nobody can hear. The hallway is crowded, but kids are busy slamming lockers, looking for notebooks, and keeping their minds on their own lives. Nobody cares what we're up to. "I didn't like Meghan much — when I first met her. But once you get to know her . . ."

"She can be cool," I finish for her.

Artie nods. "She can be cool. A little insane, maybe. But . . ."

We both laugh.

"Anyway, she needs people like us, to keep her on track," Artie says.

"Yeah," I agree. "I guess so." I hold up the poster and look at it again. My name looks strange to myself, written so large and covered in glitter.

"You don't want to do it, do you?"

I feel Artie's hazel eyes on me, but I can't bear to look at her. The world goes on around us as my heart stutters and struggles to keep pumping.

"That's why you haven't done the posters." Artie's voice is quiet.

I roll up the poster and turn to face my friend. "I didn't know it. . . . I didn't realize it until you just said it. It's just —"

"Drop out," Artie tells me.

"Like it's that simple."

"It could be." Her eyes and voice are gentle, but I still feel them cut into me.

"I can't — I can't do that to Meg."

"You have to do what's right for yourself, too, Hayley. Don't you?" Artie's forehead wrinkles, like she's confused, or maybe like she's worried about me.

I know Artie's trying to help, but somehow it just seems easier to suck it up and be the vice president than to have Meghan freak and deal with the fallout. I mean — it will be kind of fun. Parts of it.

The bell rings. "Are you going to put up the posters?" Artie asks. "Or should I take them home?"

I breathe once. Twice. "I'll put them up," I say at last.

Artie just nods. I wonder if she thinks I'm a wimp, or a dummy, or a martyr, or what. But "Okay" is all she says.

Confession:
Artie's Right

One time, in fourth grade, Artie and I were walking downtown, headed to get some ice cream, and a homeless man asked me for money. He told me that he couldn't pay for his medicine. He told me that all he needed was a few more dollars.

I had a few dollars in the pocket of my shorts — enough for my ice cream.

"I'm diabetic," the man said. And I gave him the money.

He turned to Artie. "I just need a little more," he told her.

And Artie, who had the same amount of money I did, said, "Sorry."

We walked around the corner and into the ice cream store. Artie went up to the counter and ordered a medium cone of black raspberry chocolate-chip. I got a cup of water and sat at the table, wondering if the man was really going to use my money for medicine. There was no way to know — not for sure.

Artie offered me a lick of her ice cream, and I took it. But that was almost worse, because the ice cream was delicious.

That's the thing: Artie never really has a problem doing what's right for Artie.

Sometimes, that seems harsh.

But sometimes, she's the one eating the ice cream.

And I never really knew what to make of that.

Done Properly

"Gran?" Knocking softly, I poke my head beyond her bedroom door. "Did I leave my comb in here?"

"Sorry, darling?" Gran pulls off her reading glasses and looks up from the pile of brochures scattered across her bed. "Your comb?"

"I thought maybe I left it in your bathroom," I tell her as I come to perch on the corner of her mattress.

"I haven't seen it." Gran huffs a sigh and scowls at the brochures. "Of course, things are so untidy that it may be beneath all of these."

"How's the wedding planning going?" I ask.

"Atrociously. Don't let's mention it."

"That well?"

Gran places her reading glasses on the bedside table. "It was great fun the first time I did it. When I was marrying your grandfather, Gerard. But this time, it just seems like an unnecessary expense."

I trace a finger over one of the pink embroidered roses on Gran's bedspread. "You don't want to get married?"

"What? Horrors! Of course I do! I just don't want to pay for a *wedding*."

"Well — it isn't about the money, right?"

"That's the sort of thing that people say when they have a great deal of money, and very little sense," Gran says. "I happen to have a great deal of sense and little money. And I don't see why I should spend heaps of money, time, and energy on something I don't actually want."

"When you put it that way . . ."

"If I'm going to spend a great deal of money on something, it will be your education, Hayley dear. Yours and Chloe's. Or perhaps a house for your mother. But I've already had a beautiful wedding, and I don't need another. This certainly isn't my 'princess dreams come true,'" she adds, pointing to the headline on one of the brochures. She scoffs, obviously revolted by the very idea. "Of course, I don't know how to tell your mother all of that."

"Do you think she'll mind?"

"Hayley — did you know that your father and mother eloped?"

"Sure."

"They never had a proper wedding, and I think — well, it's just superstition, of course. But the divorce is so fresh in her mind. . . ." Gran leans forward to place her hand on mine. "I do think your mother wants the wedding done properly, if you see what I'm saying."

"Oh."

"And she's gone to such effort." Gran's voice is full of regret.

"True." I think this over for a moment. "Do you think it will be better to wait until she books the caterers, and *then* tell her that you don't want the wedding? Or maybe after it's all over?"

Gran closes her eyes and chuckles softly. When she opens them again, they're as brilliant as diamonds. "I think, perhaps, sooner is better than later."

"That's what I was thinking."

Gran gives me a peck on the cheek. "I'll tell her soon, darling. Thank you."

"Sleep well," I say, and I pad down the hallway to the bedroom I share with Chloe. My sister is on her bed, snuggling with Tessie.

"She can't sleep in here," I say to Chloe.

"Why not?"

"Because she wakes me up at five in the morning when she sleeps in here," I say. "Besides, that's why we have her dog bed in the living room, remember?"

Chloe pouts.

"Don't give me the big dog eyes," I implore. "You, either," I say to the dog, but neither one of them stops.

"Mom says Tessie has to go back to the shelter this weekend." Chloe is begging, her eyes filling with tears.

Rip my heart out. "Oh, Chlo." I use my gentlest voice and sit down on the bed next to her. "I'm sorry."

"No, you're not," she mutters, and I'm silent for a moment. Well, I'm not *that* sorry. But I am a *little* sorry. I pet Tessie's silky ears.

"We knew she would have to go back someday," I say.

Chloe kisses Tessie's face, and the dog licks her face.

"She can sleep in here," I say, because I'm not really a horrible person.

I swear, that dog does not understand "sit" or "stay," but she seems to understand the entire sentence I just uttered, because she goes and curls herself up into a doughnut at the end of Chloe's bed. Chloe leans back against her pillow, and I head over to my own bed.

"Good night, Chloe," I say as I click off the light.

My little sister just rolls over, so that her back is to me.

It isn't easy when someone you love is angry with you.

But I can't always make everything perfect for everyone.

Can I?

Like a Nightmare

"Stop!" I say. "Too much! Too much!" I'm at the beach, where a dolphin is trying to touch noses. But I don't want to get my face wet. Chloe begs the dolphin to come to her, but it only wants me, and I can't get it to leave me alone. . . .

I open my eyes to darkness. The sunny beach disappears, and I realize that I'm at home, in my room. It's the middle of the night.

But my face is wet.

"Stop!" I say as Tessie licks my eyeball. "Ew!"

She whines and races to the door, then rushes back again.

"Chloe," I groan. "Your dog wants to go out."

Chloe doesn't move or make a sound. I'm telling you, that girl sleeps like a brick. Even in my groggy state, I realize that waking her up is going to be more trouble than just letting the dog out of the room, so I go to the door and open it.

Tessie races through it, skids to a stop at the end of the hallway, and then races back to me, expectantly. "Oh, ugh, do you want to go outside?" I ask her. "Now?"

She whines and jumps up on my leg, and I'm just about to turn around and go make Chloe take the dog out when the smell of smoke hits my nose.

"Is that — Ohmigosh!" Suddenly, I'm so awake that my body takes off before my brain even has time to catch up. "Chloe! Chloe! Wake up! There's a fire!"

"Mraf?" Chloe mumbles.

I shake her. "Fire! Chloe! Get up!"

"What?" She sits straight up. "Are you —" Then she must smell it, too, because she tosses back her covers and jumps out of bed.

I'm already running down with the hall with Tessie prancing at my ankles as Mom comes out of her bedroom, pulling on a robe. "Hayley?"

"Mom, there's a fire!" I dash into Gran's room. "Gran! Smoke."

Gran gets up, calm as can be. "Thank you, dear," she says.

"Mother!" Mom races into Gran's bedroom. "We've got to hurry!"

"Yes, dear, of course," Gran says, putting on her slippers.

"Mother, there's no time for that!" Mom insists, but Gran just says that she's not about to risk getting a cold, and then she goes to her closet and pulls out a box. "Mother!" Mom cries. "What are you doing? What is that? Leave it!"

"Absolutely not," Gran says. "It's important documents and a photo album."

"We've got to get out of here!" Chloe wails as Tessie runs around her in a circle, like a herding dog.

"All right, all right," Gran says, and we all grab our coats and boots and hurry down the back stairs — Tessie leading the way.

The moment we open the door, we're smacked with the sound of a blaring horn mingled with a wailing siren. Red lights flicker against the brick walls as we hurry around the block, to the front of the Tea Room.

"It's the flower shop!" Chloe cries, and she's right — some of the firefighters are pointing a hose at Malik's Fine Flowers. But the real fire is next door, at the new Mexican restaurant.

"Oh, my —" My voice is strangled, and it's hard to breathe. The air is thick with smoke; a black cloud pours into the gray sky. It's amazing — it's a cool spring night, but you wouldn't know it. It's like standing before a massive bonfire — my hair rises in the heat. We all watch, stunned, as a group of firefighters aim a hose at the flaming windows.

The image blurs as my eyes fill. *The flower shop! And what about our home? What about the café?*

"Get back!" one of the firefighters shouts at us, and we retreat a few steps.

"Umer always said the venting wasn't done properly," Gran murmurs. "Oh, how horrible!" She puts a hand over her mouth.

Another fire truck pulls up. Then another. Now the whole street is flickering in the red lights. With their helmets and jackets and gear, all the firefighters look alike, and the street seems to be swarming with them. Northampton doesn't have this many trucks — they must be coming from nearby towns. People have come out of their homes to watch.

Mom stops a firefighter who is hurrying past. "Excuse me," she says quickly. "Will the surrounding buildings be all right?"

"It looks like the fire's contained for now, ma'am," he says, and I feel us all sink with relief. "But I wouldn't head inside, if that's what you were thinking."

"That is *not* what she was thinking," Gran assures him before he hurries off. "Absolutely not!"

"At least there aren't any apartments above the stores," Mom says, pulling Gran close. Our building has apartments, but there's a tattoo parlor over the flower shop and a dance studio over the restaurant. Nobody is ever inside those buildings in the middle of the night. "I hope no one was hurt."

"And *we're* okay," I add. I reach for Chloe's hand, and we lace our fingers together. She snuggles against me, and then leans down to pat the dog.

"Tessie saved us!" Chloe crows.

We all stare at the dog, who is standing there, tail wagging.

Mom puts a hand to her forehead. "I think I need to sit down," she says.

And at the word *sit*, Tessie does.

Can you believe that?

"Good dog," Chloe says. She kneels down and hugs Tessie, who goes mad licking her face. "Good, good dog! *Best* dog!"

I really can't disagree with her there.

Confession:
Dog Pros and Cons

*C*ons:

- Pees on posters
- Chews sweaters
- Fur on everything
- Dog breath
- Poop bags
- Slobber
- Has to go for a walk, even when hail is falling from the sky like it's Armageddon
- Doesn't speak English

Pros:

• Saved us from a fire

• Best dog ever

I don't think that dog is going anywhere.

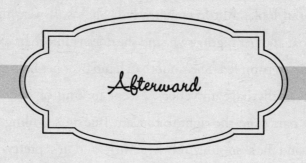

Afterward

"It still smells a bit smoky in here," Mom says as she opens the window at the end of the living room. "Ugh, now that's making it worse." She shuts it again.

It's six in the morning. The firefighters worked for three hours to put out the blaze. When it was over, the restaurant was pretty much a smoking ruin. The whole street stinks of smoke.

"Never mind," Gran says, crossing to the back window. "We're very lucky, and this will all air out quickly."

The doorbell rings, and Mom pulls it open to reveal a very worried-looking Mr. Malik. "Esther!" he cries. "Oh, thank heavens you're all right!"

He hurries to my grandmother and gives her a warm hug.

Gran looks a little embarrassed. She's still wearing her overcoat and her nightgown, and she doesn't like to be caught looking so rumpled. She smooths a hand over her hair, which doesn't really have any effect, except to kind of switch the messy part from the right to the left. But she's smiling up at him, and he's smiling down at her, and it's pretty cute, actually.

"But the flower shop!" Chloe cries.

"Oh, don't worry about that, Chloe dear," Mr. Malik tells her. "I have insurance." He takes both of Gran's hands and squeezes them. Then he looks around at all of us. "Everything I truly care about is unharmed."

Mom makes him sit down on the couch and then offers everyone some tea. I go to the kitchen and put a few leftover cupcakes onto a plate. Why not, right? I mean, a cupcake is just a muffin with frosting, and it's after six in the morning. Breakfast.

When I come back into the living room, Mr. Malik is saying, "Yes, yes. It's true. This will be very hard on the business, I'm afraid." He turns to me. "Oh, thank you, Hayley, these look lovely. I will take one, thank you very much." He looks at Gran very seriously. "My dear, I'm afraid I have something very difficult to tell you."

"Yes?" she asks.

"Well, I'm afraid that the wedding will have to be put off for a while," he admits. "You know, these insurance companies can take a while with the payments, and the flower shop will have to be renovated. The café wasn't harmed, was it?"

"Just a bit of smoke damage," Gran tells him. "Nothing worth speaking of. I might have to replace a few chairs."

"Well, the flower shop will need quite a bit of work, which means that I think our wedding will have to be . . . postponed, you see. There simply isn't time to plan much."

Gran's eyebrows fly up, and she glances over at me.

"I hope you aren't terribly disappointed," Mr. Malik says.

Gran smiles a smile that reaches up to her eyes, which sparkle like stars. "The blessing of a tragedy," she tells him, "is that it puts your life into perspective."

"Yes," he agrees. "It makes it easy to remember what's important. Don't you agree, Hayley?"

I look at Chloe, who is cuddling Tessie on the couch. My mother comes in with a tray loaded with teacups and a teapot. She's rumpled and tired and her hair is sticking out madly, but she still looks beautiful to me. The soft light gathers at the window, illuminating the room — the carpet with the torn corner, the couch with the hole at the arm, the nicked coffee table — making it look cozy. I love everyone in this room.

I love them so much.

"I think we're very lucky," I say, and everyone agrees.

And then we all have cupcakes for breakfast.

Lady's Slippers

"Come on!" Chloe shouts as she hurries ahead, leaping from one railroad tie to another. We're hiking a trail with Dad and Annie, and this part is a little marshy. The railroad ties serve as a makeshift bridge through the spring muck. Above us, the trees are still stark, but small fiddleheads are uncurling at their feet. The air is chilly but not uncomfortable as we walk. "I see a lady's slipper!" Chloe shouts over her shoulder.

Annie hurries to catch up with Chloe, and they trek off the path a bit on the other side of the marsh. Dead leaves and sticks crash at every footstep.

Dad and I don't rush. We just pick our way slowly after them.

"How's your Gran?" Dad asks. "Is everything all right after the fire?"

"It's fine," I tell him. "There wasn't much damage at all." I explain about Mr. Malik's shop, though, and Dad says it's too bad.

We're quiet for a few moments, and finally I know that if I don't say it now, I never will. "Dad," I say slowly, "I don't want to go to Islip Academy."

He's silent for a moment. I think I really surprised him. "Why not?"

"I just — don't. It doesn't feel right."

"But it's such a good school," Dad says. "They're grooming the leaders of tomorrow!" That's right out of the catalog, by the way.

"But what if I don't want to be a leader of tomorrow?" I ask him. "What if I just want to be a normal kid of today?"

Dad steps off the railroad tie and down onto solid earth. The path winds ahead of us, disappearing into the woods. It makes me think of this poem I read once, by Robert Frost. It's about two paths in the woods, and choosing which one to walk on. I guess a lot of stuff in life is like that. You have to make choices. And for everything you choose, there's stuff you give up.

And there's stuff you gain.

"They have a great science program." Dad is still talking about Islip Academy. "And the arts."

"Dad, I know. It's fancier, that's for sure. But I have really great teachers, and I think that's the most important thing. Besides, baking cupcakes is my favorite extracurricular activity. I don't want to give that up to do photography, or Irish step dancing, or whatever."

"But Irish step dancing is beautiful," Dad argues.

"I know, Dad, but —"

"Hayley, I'm teasing you." Dad takes my hand. "I mean, I do like Irish step dancing. But you shouldn't do it if you don't want to. And I'm not going to make you go to school anywhere you really don't want to go. I just want you to get a good education."

"I'm getting a good education. In fact, Señor Derby has already started us on ninth-grade Spanish." And then, before I can stop myself, I say, "Which costs one hundred thirty dollars, by the way."

Dad nods. "Right," he says, as if the memory has been lurking at the back of his mind, and suddenly jumped out at him. "Right — I think your mom mentioned it."

I want to say that I know she did, but I don't.

"I think I owe her for the dentist, too," Dad adds.

"You should talk to her about it, maybe," I suggest.

There's a crash and an *ouch!* and then Annie appears, followed by Chloe, who races past her and back onto the trail. "We found a whole bunch of lady's slippers!" Chloe cries.

"I had never seen one before!" Annie exclaims. "They're so pretty!" She's looking very dressed down in yoga pants, a short parka, and bright blue running shoes. I remember the first time we went apple picking with Annie. She wore high heels that got stuck in the mud. She's come a long way since then.

"Come on," Chloe urges as she plunges back into the woods, "I'll show you where they are! Not far!"

Dad puts his hand on my shoulder and we start after Annie and Chloe, leaving the beaten path behind us.

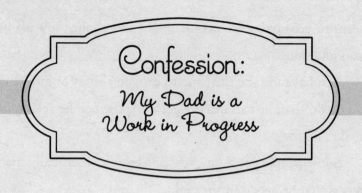

Confession: My Dad is a Work in Progress

When I was eight years old, I bought my father a tiepin for his birthday. It was gold — well, gold-plated, anyway — and shaped like a duck. I had wanted to get him something nice, and I had saved my allowance for over a month to get it. When he opened it, he said, "Why a duck?"

I told him that it was because I thought it was cute. And my father said, "A gift should really show that you put some time into thinking about what the person would like."

That was all he said.

And I never saw him wear the tiepin.

Here is the thing about my dad: He isn't a bad person. Not really. He just acts like it sometimes. He doesn't always seem to get how other people might feel about the stuff he says and does.

You have to take the time to explain things to him. But if you do that, he can usually get it. And when he gets it, he makes up for it.

Some people get it quicker. But I guess what really matters is that he gets it in the end.

Honey-Sesame Cupcakes

(makes approximately 12 cupcakes)

Have you ever had those little sesame candies that they sell in Asian food stores? I love them! These are inspired by their subtle, almost caramely flavor.

INGREDIENTS:

- 1/2 cup white sesame seeds
- 1-1/4 cups gluten-free flour
- 3/4 teaspoon baking powder
- 1/2 teaspoon baking soda
- 1/2 teaspoon salt
- 3/4 cup milk
- 3/4 teaspoon apple cider vinegar
- 3/4 cup honey
- 1 teaspoon vanilla extract
- 1/3 cup canola oil
- 2 tablespoons black sesame seeds

INSTRUCTIONS:

1. Preheat the oven to 350°F. Line a muffin pan with cupcake liners.

2. Place a skillet over medium heat, then add the white sesame seeds to toast them, constantly stirring and watching until they start to brown. Immediately remove the skillet from the heat and place the seeds into a bowl to cool.

3. In a large bowl, sift together the flour, baking powder, baking soda, and salt.

4. In a separate bowl, stir together the milk and apple cider vinegar, and let sit to curdle a bit. Once good and curdled, add the honey, vanilla extract, and oil.

5. With a whisk or handheld mixer, add the dry ingredients to the wet ones a little bit at a time, stopping to scrape the sides of the bowl a few times, and mix until no lumps remain. Then mix in the black sesame seeds and 1/4 cup of the toasted white sesame seeds, conserving the rest for the frosting.

6. Fill cupcake liners two-thirds of the way and bake for 20–22 minutes. Transfer to a cooling rack, and let cool completely before frosting.

Sesame Buttercream Frosting

INGREDIENTS:

1/4 cup sesame seeds (from the toasted batch)

1 cup butter, softened

3-1/2 cups confectioners' sugar

1–2 tablespoons milk

1 teaspoon vanilla extract

INSTRUCTIONS:

1. In a small food processor, or with a mortar and pestle, grind the remaining 1/4 cup of toasted white sesame seeds until pulverized into a powder.

2. In a large bowl, with an electric mixer, cream the butter until it's lighter in color, about 2–3 minutes.

3. Slowly beat in the confectioners' sugar in 1/2-cup batches, adding a little bit of milk whenever the frosting becomes too thick. Add the vanilla extract and ground sesame seeds and continue mixing on high speed for about 3–7 minutes, until the frosting is light and fluffy.

The Candidate

"Hey, Hayley," Omar says as he puts a five-dollar bill on the counter. "Could I get a honey sesame cupcake?"

"Sure — I just made them," I tell him as I pull one out of the case and place it on a plate.

"It looks great." He looks around the café, which has cheery new striped curtains and new comfortable chairs where the old upholstered couch used to be. "I like the new seats you guys have in here." He climbs onto a stool and takes a bite of frosting as I ring up the sale.

"We had to replace a few things that were smelling too much like a chimney," I explain.

"What a mess," Omar says. "I can't believe the restaurant burned down."

"The two guys in Boston who owned it aren't going to rebuild. Mr. Malik says that the building owner doesn't want them back. He's going to renovate the space and rent it out to someone else."

"That's good. Too bad about the flower shop."

"I know." I wipe a few crumbs from the counter. I don't like talking about the flower shop. I feel so sad every time I pass by it, all boarded up. "But it looks like we'll keep Tessie now," I say to shake off the gloom that has settled over me. I explain how she saved us.

Omar laughs. "I always knew you'd keep that dog," he says. "It was love at first sight."

"I didn't really feel that way," I admit.

"Oh, I meant that the dog loved you guys," Omar explains. Then he sighs. "I really love working with the dogs. Too bad I may have to leave that job."

"Why?"

"My mom doesn't want me to fall behind in my grades, so she says I have to choose two activities. It's class president, my volunteer work, and sports. I won't give up baseball. And there's no way I'll turn down president if I win, so — it's kind of an easy decision."

"Oh."

"Are you going to keep working here, if you win?"

I look around the café. Light is making the white curtains glow, and the dark wood floor gleam. "I want to. But Meghan has about fifty thousand things planned, so I'll probably have to cut down."

Omar finishes the cupcake and pushes himself off the stool. "Well, maybe you won't have to choose . . . or maybe we'll lose, and you will," he says cheerfully. "Are you ready for the speeches tomorrow?"

"Uh, almost," I say. I tell myself that this is not a lie, because I still have time to write a speech tonight. And then I *will* be ready. So I'm "almost" there, right? "Are you?"

"I think I wrote a pretty good one, if I do say so myself." Omar smiles mischievously. But he always smiles like that, so sometimes it's hard to know if he's up to something or not. "See you tomorrow, Hayley," he says.

"See you," I say as he pushes against the door and steps out into the bright sunshine.

It seems wrong to want to lose something. But I can't help it.

Speech

"And our plans for a . . . for a . . . oh, ugh!" I'm trying to remember as much of my campaign speech as I can without glancing at my notes, but I'm having trouble. A lot of trouble. Like, I can't remember anything, which is amazing, given that I wrote it myself. I look at the note card in my hand. It isn't easy to try to read it and walk down the hallway at the same time. "Right! For a day in which the whole school can come together to beautify — oh, shoot! I'll never remember this stupid thing!"

Marco appears out of the sea of students around me. Everyone is moving in a single mass toward the auditorium to hear the campaign speeches. The hallway is echoing with chatter and shouts, shuffling feet and general chaos. He smiles at me. "Are you ready for the speeches?"

"Aaarrgh!"

"That good?"

"This is hopeless," I say. "I'll never memorize it in time. The speeches start in seven minutes!"

"Just read from your notes," Marco suggests. "Everyone does that. Look up once in a while. It doesn't have to be perfect."

I don't mention that I promised Meghan that I would have the speech memorized. I really meant to. But — it turns out that it's really hard to remember things. "Okay, talk to me about something else," I command as I tuck the cards into my backpack. "Anything!" And the minute I say that, I worry that he'll bring up the barbecue, but he doesn't.

"Um — I think I might take that photography class at Islip," Marco says.

"Really? You think your dad will pay for it?"

Marco digs his fists into the pockets of his gray corduroys and hunches a little as he walks. "He's insisting that I need work experience. He'll probably let me take the class if I can find a job or volunteer gig."

An idea occurs to me. "I might know of one," I say, and I tell him about Omar and the job at the shelter.

"Well, in that case, I guess I'd better vote for Omar for president," Marco says. He's smiling, and I can't tell if he's joking or not, but I don't have a chance to ask because Meghan comes barreling over and wraps me in an excited hug.

"Speechies!" she crows. "Are you ready?"

"I didn't manage to memorize it," I admit.

"I didn't memorize mine, either," Meghan announces, waving her hand. "Don't worry about it." She stops and looks at me more closely. "You aren't worried, are you?"

"No," I say, but Marco puts in, "She's freaked," and of course Meghan listens to Marco.

"Don't freak," she says, giving my arm a squeeze. "I will love you no matter what."

"Even if I forget everything?" I ask. "Even if I run crying from the podium?"

"Even if your pants fall off," Meghan promises.

"That's love," Marco says.

Meghan interlaces her fingers with mine and warms my cold hand in hers. "No matter what," she says again.

And the thing about Meghan is — I know she means it.

I know it for sure, and I wonder how I ever could have doubted it.

The next moment, we push through the auditorium doors. I scan my notes frantically as everyone takes their seats and the principal starts to talk about the campaign, and civic duty, and democracy, and blah, blah, blah. I'm feeling the way I feel every time I get on a roller coaster — the bar goes down and I'm furious that I let someone talk me into this. And then we start out, up . . . up . . . up . . . and there's that pause at the top when you're filled with the worst sort of dread and you know you've made a horrible mistake.

Why do people ever go on roller coasters?

I'm reading my speech, but all I can think is, *I don't want to do this. I don't want to.*

I don't want to.

There isn't a speech for class treasurer, since the only person running is Tanisha Osborne, and she's the smartest girl in the whole school, so she can definitely be trusted with the job, even if she's a little stuck up.

Then Ashley Oakes gives her speech for secretary. Amber Olson gives her speech for secretary next. It's funny how two girls with similar names and similar hairstyles both want the same job. Either one of them is fine with me. They both have great handwriting — and good keyboarding skills.

And then the principal says, "Hayley Hicks, running for eighth-grade class vice president," and a few people clap politely as I stand up, and I feel the click, click, click of rising to the top of the roller coaster. I walk down the aisle and up the steps to the stage. Click, click, click, click, click . . .

I feel like a robot, or like an empty shell as I step up to the podium. It's an out-of-body experience, like — I'm doing these things, but I'm not even really there. I place my notes on the podium and look out at the audience. Then I smile, the way Gran coached me.

There, in the third row, is Meghan. She's sitting next to my empty seat. She grins at me, and gives me a thumbs-up.

She'll love me no matter what, I think.

I think about Artie. And I think about Gran, and the wedding she didn't want to have.

I lower the microphone and lean forward.

"Friends and classmates," I say, speaking as slowly and carefully as I can. "I've decided not to run for vice president."

Confession:
Overdue

Three years ago, I checked out five books on elephants for a report I was writing. *Asian Elephants in their Natural Habitats* was one. I forget the others. But I remember that one because it was on the top of the pile.

The pile that sat under my bed for almost a year.

What happened was that they were overdue. They were overdue by a couple of weeks when I remembered them, but I couldn't bear to bring them back. I thought that the librarian would be angry at me. I thought she'd yell, and that she wouldn't let me check out any more books. And, later, I thought that it would cost hundreds of dollars in fines to return them. So I just never went to the library.

And I let the books sit under my bed.

But I didn't forget about them. No. Actually, I thought about them a lot. Every night, I checked under my bed to make sure that they were still there, and they always were. And I would think, *This weekend, I'll take them back to the library.* But I never would. I'd just feel queasy and make up excuses.

Until one day, my mother found the books while she was tidying my room. And that weekend, we returned them. Heart hammering, I pushed the books across the counter and started the speech I had rehearsed at home. "I'm sorry these books are so late —" I began as the librarian zapped them with her scanner.

"Okay. Twelve dollars and fifty cents, please," she said to my mother, and my mother paid the money and that was the end of it.

Almost a year of feeling sick over those books.

I still sometimes wake up and think, *I have to return those books this weekend!* And then I remember that they're returned — it's all finished, and my head swims with relief.

Almost a year for something that was over in a heartbeat.

Just like that.

From the Phone Files:
Part 3

"Hayley? Oh my gosh, I can't believe you backed out today!"

"Artie?"

"Yeah, it's me. Wow. Just — wow."

"I know — I don't know what happened. That wasn't what I planned to say at all! I just went up there —"

"I'm impressed."

"Wait — you are?"

"Remember the library books?"

"Ugh."

"Aren't you happy you just got up there and told the truth? Like, the truth will set you free?"

"Well . . . it set me free. . . ."

"Is Meg freaking?"

"She was really nice about it, but I think she's pretty disappointed."

"Yeah. She'll get over it, though."

"You think?"

"Are you kidding? She thinks you're the coolest."

"She does?"

"Hayley — isn't she one of your best friends?"

"Yeah."

"Well, then. Duh!"

"It just didn't make sense to be unhappy for a year just because I couldn't deal with telling Meghan the truth. She actually said she was sorry for putting so much pressure on me to run."

"See? You did the right thing."

"I just wish I hadn't waited so long to do it."

"Pobody's nerfect."

"Right. Pobody's nerfect."

"Go make some cupcakes. You'll feel better."

"Thanks, Artie."

"Sure."

"And thanks for calling."

"Sure, Hayley. I'm glad I did."

Something New

"Those are pretty," Chloe says as I frost a white flower at the top of a vanilla cupcake.

"I've been practicing the flowers," I explain. "So that I'll be ready for the wedding."

"If there is one." Chloe sounds gloomy, and Rupert pats her hand. It's so funny how he's like a little old man, sometimes.

"Where will you put them?" Rupert asks, bending his head to peer into the display case. "It looks pretty full in there."

"Gran says it's a special order," I tell him.

"Is that why the Tea Room is closed this morning?" Chloe asks. "I've already seen a few sad-eyed college students peeking in the window. I feel bad for them."

"There are plenty of places to get a latte in this town," I tell her. It's a cloudy, cold Saturday, and a few late spring snow flurries are drifting across the sky. I'm tired of the cold, but I always feel a thrill when I see snow falling. Even when it isn't welcome.

Mr. Malik taps at the door, and Chloe rushes to unlock it. "Good morning!" he greets us, and his whole face is one enormous smile.

"You're drowning in flowers!" Chloe says. He really is — he has one large bouquet and several smaller ones. "Where did you get them?"

"From the wholesaler!" Mr. Malik says. "It was a marvelous deal, and I couldn't resist brightening the café a bit. You don't mind, do you?"

"We love it!" Chloe says.

"And yellow roses are Gran's favorite," I tell him.

"Are they, really?" Mr. Malik says with the twinkliest eyes I've ever seen.

"Hello, my dears!" Gran sings as she bustles in from the back office. "My dear Mr. Malik, how well you look today!"

"And you are simply lovely," Mr. Malik tells her as they hold each other's hands.

"You two do look nice," Chloe says.

"Yeah — what's up?" I ask. Gran is wearing her lavender suit, and Mr. Malik has on his blue one, with a lavender tie. "Did you guys call each other so that you could be all matchy-matchy?" I joke.

"Hayley, darling, there's no need to put those cupcakes in a box," Gran tells me. "Just place them on a plate."

At that moment, there's another knock at the locked door, and Rupert rushes to let in Uzma and a cheerful-looking woman with spiky hair. In her brown flowy dress, she looks a little bit like a pinecone.

"Hello!" I say to the pinecone lady. "Are these cupcakes for you?"

"I hope so," the woman replies. "At least one of them."

Uzma gives Rupert an affectionate kiss, and he smiles and looks at the floor, embarrassed. She just loves clucking over him.

"What's going on?" Mom asks as she walks in. "Oh — Mr. Malik! Did you bring the flowers? They're beautiful!"

He takes a medium-sized bouquet and gives it to my mother. "For you, my dear," he tells her.

"Let me just get a vase," Mom says, starting back toward the office.

"No need of that," Gran tells her. "Just hold them a moment yet." Then she strides over to the door and flips the lock closed. She gestures to the pinecone lady. "My dears, I would like to introduce you all to the Reverend Janet Bliss. Mr. Malik and I are getting married."

Chloe lets out a gasp.

"Now?" I ask.

Mr. Malik hands me a small but very beautiful bouquet of yellow and white roses. "Now, my dear." He gives another small bouquet to Chloe, and a larger one to Uzma, who is teary-eyed and smiling.

"What?" Mom cries. "Here? In the Tea Room?"

"Yes, of course, dear," Gran says. "This is where we have spent many happy hours, and neither one of us wants a fuss."

"Wait! Do you mean these cupcakes are for your wedding?" I cry. "But I wanted to make you a real cake!"

"Well, dear, keep practicing," Gran says. "I'm sure you'll get a chance someday. There's always Chloe."

Mom sits down heavily on a chair. "But — but — what about Denise? You wouldn't just get married without your other daughter, would you?"

And at that very moment, someone taps on the door. It's Officer Ramon . . . and my aunt Denise.

Chloe and Rupert rush to let them in, and then there's hugging and smiling and kissing, and my aunt even picks me up and swings me around. She works out.

And finally, we've all settled down, and Mr. Malik has given Aunt Denise a really lovely bouquet, and we all gather in a circle while Officer Ramon flips the lock again.

Gran turns to my mother. "I hope you aren't too disappointed," she says gently.

My mother's eyes are brilliant with tears, and she takes a few breaths before she can speak. "Mother — this is your wedding, not mine," she says, although I can see it isn't easy for her to talk. "All that matters is that you're happy."

"I'm happy." Gran's face looks like — well, even though there are clouds outside, and a bit of snow falling, Gran's face looks like the sun. Like it's giving off its own light. "I'm very, very happy!"

"We all are!" I say, and as I look around the room, I realize it's true. Everyone is beaming.

"And that is the best way to begin a wedding that I can think of," says the Reverend Janet Bliss.

And so we do.

Confession:
Best Wedding Ever

Two years ago, I went to my mother's cousin's wedding. There were three hundred people there. Cousin Caroline was marrying a super-rich guy, and her gown was made of French lace, beautifully cut into a mermaid tail and train. And the reception afterward was at this huge hotel. The flower arrangements were as tall as I was. Seriously. And there were two ice sculptures carved into swans.

It was like a fairy tale.

But that wedding was nothing compared to Gran's. Gran and Mr. Malik had written their own vows, and when they said them, we all blubbed our eyes out — even Officer Ramon.

And afterward, there was tea and cupcakes, and cappuccinos for Mom and Aunt Denise. Mr. Malik and Gran made an even bigger announcement — they're going to tear down the wall between the Tea Room and the flower shop, and make something new. It will be a Tea Room and bookstore.

"That way," Gran explained, "we can read poetry and sip tea whenever we like."

When she said that, I remembered the line from the poem she loves so much:

> Remember that beneath the snow and ice,
> A world awaits, till winter's fury spent.

A world awaits.

I know my mom thinks it's a jinx not to have a proper wedding. But I think this was proper, all right.

Very proper.

White-Chocolate Almond Wedding Cupcakes

(makes approximately 8 regular cupcakes
and 8 mini cupcakes)

I will never be caught off guard again! Here's a cupcake that looks like a teeny-tiny wedding cake ... but is much, much easier to make. No lazy Susan required!

INGREDIENTS:
    1 cup plus 2 tablespoons all-purpose flour
    1/3 cup almond meal
    1-1/2 teaspoons baking powder
    1/2 teaspoon salt
    2/3 cup milk
    2/3 teaspoon apple cider vinegar
    3-1/2 ounces almond paste (not marzipan), at room temperature
    1/3 cup granulated sugar
    1/3 cup canola oil

1 teaspoon vanilla extract

1 teaspoon almond extract

INSTRUCTIONS:

1. Preheat the oven to 350°F. Line a regular muffin pan with cupcake liners and spray a mini muffin pan with vegetable oil cooking spray.

2. In a large bowl, sift together the flour, almond meal, baking powder, and salt.

3. In a small bowl, stir together the milk and apple cider vinegar, and let curdle for a few minutes. While the milk is curdling, break apart the almond paste into small pieces. Then place them in a food processor along with the sugar. Process the two together until the mixture resembles wet sand. Add the oil, curdled milk, vanilla extract, and almond extract, and combine completely.

4. With your handheld mixer, add the wet ingredients to the dry ones in small batches,

stopping to scrape the sides of the bowl a few times, and mix until no lumps remain.

5. Fill the regular cupcake liners and mini muffin tin spaces two-thirds of the way (you may have additional batter, so make as many pairs of regular and mini as you can, then use up the additional in a leftover cupcake). Bake for 20–22 minutes, or when a toothpick inserted in the center of each cupcake comes out clean. Transfer to a cooling rack, and let cool completely before frosting.

TO ASSEMBLE THE CUPCAKES:

1. With a small paring knife, flatten the rounded tops of the mini cupcakes by cutting them off. You can also cut around the sides to make them straight and not angled, but that's up to you. Then cut off the tops of the regular-sized cupcakes to make them flat.

2. Frost each regular-sized cupcake and make it smooth. Set the mini cupcake on top of the

regular cupcake and carefully frost the sides, then top, so that the completed cupcake resembles a two-tiered mini wedding cake. Continue with all cupcakes until assembled, and then decorate as you would a wedding cake, with sprinkles and piped frosting, or keep it simple and delicious!

White-Chocolate Buttercream Frosting

INGREDIENTS:

1 cup butter, softened

2-1/2 cups confectioners' sugar

Up to 1/4 cup full-fat milk, heavy whipping cream, or non-dairy creamer

1/4 teaspoon vanilla extract

6 ounces high quality white chocolate, melted and cooled

INSTRUCTIONS:

1. In a large bowl, with an electric mixer, cream the butter until it's a lighter color, about 2–3 minutes.

2. Slowly beat in the confectioners' sugar in 1/2-cup batches, adding a little bit of milk whenever the frosting becomes too thick. Add the vanilla extract and melted white chocolate, and mix on high speed for about 3–7 minutes, until the frosting is light and fluffy.

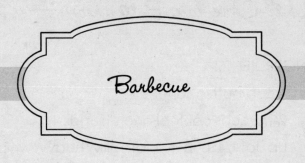

Barbecue

"You look really pretty," Marco tells me as we walk across the grass toward the covered shed.

"Thanks," I say, feeling awkward. I'm wearing a long skirt and tall boots, and a chunky sweater. The snow has completely melted away, and the evening is cool, but not cold. Smoke rises from the grills, and big outdoor heaters have been set up in the corners of the shed. I'm holding a large cupcake carrier, but I have a free arm. "Can I help you with that?"

"I've got it." Marco is pulling along a chest full of ice. Luckily, the cooler has wheels — I'm sure it's heavy. It took both Marco and Mom working together to get it out of the car. "Where do you think I should put it?"

"Let's ask the expert," I say.

Meghan is in the far corner, arranging some streamers. And she's not alone.

"Hey, Omar," Marco says as we walk up. "What are you doing?"

"Trying to make sure that Meg doesn't break her neck," Omar explains. He's holding a stepladder.

"How am I supposed to get down?" Meghan wails.

"Why did you go up there in the first place?" I demand. "You're afraid of ladders!"

"Because I had to put up the streamers!" Meghan insists.

"Why don't you think for a minute before you just climb up on something?" I ask her.

"Because I usually think of it afterward!" Meghan replies. "Isn't someone going to help me?"

"Just take one step at a time," Omar tells her. "Or jump! You're only a couple of feet off the ground."

"Jump? Are you insane? I'll fracture a limb! I'll break my n —" And she screams and flails as Omar grabs her, throws her over his shoulder, and plants her on the ground.

Bug-eyed, Meghan just stands there hyperventilating for a minute. "Gah! What! Was! That! Are! You! Nuts!" She gives him a whack with each word.

Omar holds up his arms as she smacks him. But I don't think he's hurt, as he can't stop laughing. "Meghan! You're going to have to learn to trust me if we're going to work together!"

Meghan stops her flailing and stands there, still breathing hard.

"You two are going to work together?" I ask.

"Oh, boy," Marco says.

"I've decided not to run for class president," Omar explains.

I'm surprised. "Oh."

"He's going to run for vice president, instead," Meghan announces. "I spoke to the school office, and they'll change the ballots in time for Tuesday's election."

"Wow!" Marco says. "That's great!"

"But won't you two kill each other?" I ask, then wince. Maybe I shouldn't have said that out loud.

But Meghan just laughs. "Give me a little credit, Hayley," she says, as Artie walks over.

"It looks great!" Artie gushes. "Brilliant move to get the heaters!"

"And it was brilliant of you to do all the centerpieces!" Meghan gestures to the piles of cute stuffed animals —

frogs, ducks, and turtles — arranged on the tables. "They're adorbs!"

"We're donating them to the family shelter after the party," Artie explains. "Along with some other baby and little kid supplies. Diapers and stuff. We raised a lot of money from ticket sales, and we got Salamander Café to donate all the food. Except for the cupcakes, of course," she adds, nodding to my carrier.

"Thanks to Artie!" Meghan says. She and Artie smile at each other, but I don't feel jealous. Not really. They may get along — but I know that Meghan is my real friend. And I don't think she'll ever like Artie more than she likes me.

"Where do you want this, by the way?" Marco asks, gesturing to the cooler.

"Oh, could you and Hayley go set up the drinks table?" Meghan says. "Out in front."

Marco and I walk over to where cups have already been laid out. I lay out the cupcakes, and then help Marco put bottles into the cooler.

"Artie's grown up a lot lately," he says slowly, "hasn't she? She isn't so full of herself."

"I think she just needed to figure things out," I say. "You

know — Marco . . ." I hesitate, unsure whether to say any-thing. After all, if Artie wanted him to know, she would have said something herself. But in the end, I think Marco should know. "Marco, I never sent that Islip information to your mom," I say. "I think Artie did."

"Oh." Marco stares down at one of the bottles. "I thought you did it."

He looks up at me.

"She . . . cares about you," I say. I don't think it's too much. I hope not.

"Don't you?" he asks.

"Not . . ." It's like wrestling something huge — something terrifying — to say it. But I have to. "Not the same way." I'm hot all over — hot the way I was the night of the fire.

For a long time, Marco just stands there, watching me burn.

"Okay," he says at last.

I wish I could say something that would make it all bet-ter. "You're one of the most important people in the world to me, Marco," I whisper. I think about the time he took a break from our friendship. That felt like walking around without an arm, with part of myself missing. I don't want to go through that again.

"You're important to me, too, Hayley." Marco's eyes are as deep as the ocean. "You always will be."

"Come on, you guys!" Meghan calls, gesturing from the food line. "Get a plate before it's all gone!"

The spell between me and Marco is broken, disappearing on the air. He gives me a lopsided smile, and I wave at Meghan. "Save us a seat!" I call.

"You coming?" I ask Marco. He has a faraway look on his face.

"I think I just want to do something first," he says. "I'll be there in a second." Then he leans over and kisses me. On the forehead. It's a gentle, brotherly kiss, and the feel of his lips linger for a moment.

"What's that for?" I ask.

"For being a good friend," he says. "And for being honest." Then he walks away, toward the table where Artie is sitting with Omar and Meghan.

I stand there with a fluttering heart for a few moments. Finally, I manage to walk over to the food line. Emma Sawyer, Allison Beale, and Noelle Sanchez get in line behind me. Then comes Kyle, so I let the others go ahead. "Hey, Kyle," I say.

"Oh — hey, Hayley! Hey. How's it going?"

"Pretty good." I explain about Meghan and Omar — how they've finally made peace. Sort of. We talk as we move slowly past the buffet. I put some chicken onto my plate, then some onto his. I know it's hard for him to do that stuff for himself. Then I tell him about Gran's wedding.

"Got any leftover cupcakes?" Kyle jokes.

"I made some for dessert." I start toward Meghan's table, and turn back suddenly. "Who are you sitting with?" I ask. "Do you want to come sit with me and my friends?"

Kyle is pale-skinned, and when he blushes, he turns a beautiful shade of pink. "Aren't you — aren't you sitting with Marco?"

"I'm sitting with lots of people," I tell him.

"I don't want to just — wedge myself in," he says carefully.

"It's not like that at all," I say. "I *want* to sit with you."

Yes — I said that. That's the kind of thing I can say to Kyle. I don't know why, but it's easy to be honest with him.

And he smiles the most wonderful smile. "Okay," he says.

So I lead him to the table where Artie and Marco are laughing over something. Artie looks at me and smiles shyly.

She and Marco used to be good friends. I don't know if there will ever be any romance between them, but I'm glad to see they're talking again. No matter what, the three of us grew up together. Our childhoods overlap.

We're almost like family.

Meghan pulls up an extra chair for Kyle, not even pausing in her argument with Omar. It's something about how they might organize a book drive. They don't sound angry, though. It's more like they're really enjoying it. Kyle sits down beside me.

"I can't believe the school year is almost over," Kyle says. "Just a few more weeks, and then seventh grade will be over."

"But a lot of new stuff is beginning," I say.

Kyle smiles and nods, and a blond curl spills over his large gray eyes. "I hope so," he says.

I give him a playful nudge against the shoulder. But he doesn't move away. Instead, we just sit there, letting our shoulders touch lightly as we talk some more, ignoring our dinners.

Who knew that a barbecue could be one of life's greatest moments?

But it can.

Trust me — it can.

Acknowledgments

I would like to gratefully acknowledge the help of my sister, Zoë Papademetriou, who created the recipes in this book. I would also like to thank my editor Anamika Bhatnagar for her insight and input, and my agent Rosemary Stimola for her unwavering enthusiasm. Huge thanks to Cassandra Pelham, Starr Mayo, and Jackie Hornberger, whose help and high standards are essential to this series. As always, a loving hug to my husband and daughter. Thank you to Nerissa Nields for her support of my blog, and to Ellen Wittlinger, Nancy Werlin, Liza Ketchum, and Pat Collins for their willingness to share their work and careful attention to mine. And a huge shout-out to my fellow writers (and friends) at Vermont College of Fine Arts!